I0684607

WHILE SHE SLEEPS

Amanda Crum

www.BOROUGHSPUBLISHINGGROUP.com

PUBLISHER'S NOTE: This is a work of fiction. Names, characters, places and incidents either are the product of the author's imagination or are used fictitiously. Any resemblance to actual events, locales, business establishments or persons, living or dead, is coincidental. Boroughs Publishing Group does not have any control over and does not assume responsibility for author or third-party websites, blogs or critiques or their content.

WHILE SHE SLEEPS
Copyright © 2021 Amanda Crum

All rights reserved. Unless specifically noted, no part of this publication may be reproduced, scanned, stored in a retrieval system or transmitted in any form or by any means, electronic, mechanical, photocopying, recording, or otherwise, known or hereinafter invented, without the express written permission of Boroughs Publishing Group. The scanning, uploading and distribution of this book via the Internet or by any other means without the permission of Boroughs Publishing Group is illegal and punishable by law. Participation in the piracy of copyrighted materials violates the author's rights.

ISBN: 978-1-953810-69-4

WHILE SHE SLEEPS

Chapter One

In the bowl of the holler, sunrise arrived this September morning in shades of indigo and citrine. With it came wisps of fog, the smell of damp mud, and the bullfrogs' bleating echoing off the hills. The morning shook off the dregs of night and was a fresh start, like the first snow.

Autumn drove through the hills, the car windows down, breathing in the heady scent of the outdoors. A thermos of hot tea with lemon and honey sat on the seat beside her. It was two hours before she had to be in the office. Driving around in the early hours before anyone else was awake was a luxury she enjoyed and used as a way to clear out the cobwebs and shake off the bad dreams.

Last night, the usual nightmares hadn't plagued her. She'd had a brief dream lacking in intensity, where she sat talking quietly with an unfamiliar little blonde girl. A Brooke-lookalike. The real Brooke Napier was only seven years old, and was one of Autumn's favorite people in the world. She was a child who'd have a bright future if Autumn had anything to say about it.

There's a shadow in you, her grandmother had told her when she was ten or eleven years old. At the time, Autumn hadn't understood what the words meant, but when she got older, she recognized the darkness in herself for what it was: a shadow casting a pall over everything she did, no matter where she went.

"Jesus," she cried out, yanking the steering wheel hard to the right as she crested a hill. Barely in time, she saw a slash of red—a flannel shirt flashing against the greenery like a handful of poppies. She'd been so deep in her thoughts, she'd taken the curves dangerously fast, not bothering to heed the speed limit because she knew the roads so well.

The man stopped walking to glare at her. He was huge, at least six foot three with a massive barrel chest and thick arms. She caught a glimpse of his dark eyes flashing with irritation before she passed him. She stopped at the top of the next hill, pulling over onto the soft, pine-needle-ridden shoulder and thought, *I need to apologize to him.*

She had to wait only a moment before he came into view. When he spotted her, he slowed his pace and glared.

"Hi," she said as she got out of the car. "I'm sorry. I didn't even see you until the last second."

"You were speeding," he said roughly, coming to a stop a few feet away. His eyes—so dark they were nearly black—drew her in. She'd had trouble making eye contact with others since childhood, and even after training herself in college to meet people's gazes, she still faltered. But not with him.

She took a moment to study him, noting the hardness of the sharp line of his jaw anchored by a dark beard. His fists were clenched at his sides, his anger almost palpable. She took a step back and felt the cold, reassuring metal of the car door against her bottom.

"I'm sorry, but you *were* walking pretty close to the road," she said, lifting her chin. She'd dealt with worse than him. "I drive these roads all the time and I've never seen anyone out this early. I wasn't expecting you."

"Next time I'll track you down and ask your permission before I go for a walk," he said, moving past her. She caught a whiff of sweat and something wild and green, as though he'd been sleeping beneath the pines.

A dozen clever comebacks whipped through her head, but she couldn't bring herself to say any of them. He was intimidating, but that wasn't it, not entirely. She'd been holding her own against angry men for years.

No, something else held her back, and she couldn't name it. There was a vague feeling of embarrassment, but why should she care what this stranger thought of her?

She watched him stride along the road, then got behind the wheel and sat in silence for a moment before starting the vehicle. By the time she maneuvered carefully over the hill, the man had disappeared.

***

"I hope you got some sleep last night," her friend Tana said when Autumn arrived at work at the state offices where she was a social worker. Tana's fingers flew over the keyboard of her computer, typing up what looked like a lengthy report. "You're gonna need it today."

"Fun morning?" Autumn asked warily, handing her colleague a cup of hot tea.

"The phone's been ringing off the hook. Everyone needs something from us. Tana nodded toward the stack of paperwork teetering in the center of Autum's desk. "Sorry about the mess. Don't let it stress you out, it's mostly stuff that needs to be filed."

Autumn sat and sipped her tea, seeing the paperwork, yet not seeing it at the same time. Her mind felt like the eye of a hurricane, a calm center surrounded by whorls of thought. It was a good thing she *had* gotten some sleep the night before, otherwise her run-in with the man in the flannel shirt would have left her grumpy for the rest of the day.

Pausing her typing Tana asked, "You okay? Nightmares again?"

"No," Autumn said softly. "For the first time in a while, I slept pretty well actually. I had a weird run-in with some guy earlier this morning, though. I can't seem to shake it."

"What happened?" Tana turned around in her chair to face Autum. "What guy?"

"I don't know, I've never seen him before. I thought I knew everyone in Pine Hollow, but I definitely wouldn't have missed this guy. He's massive. Built like a tree."

"Where'd you see him?"

"Out on Old Mill Road," Autumn said. "He was walking along the tree line. I almost hit him."

"What was he doing out there so early? Hunting?"

Autumn shook her head. "No, I don't think so. He didn't have any equipment with him. I've been driving out there at sunrise for years, and I've never seen anyone before, which is why I wasn't expecting him to be there. Especially so close to the road. I stopped and apologized, but he was pissed. Gave me attitude and walked away."

"He was alone?"

"As far as I know."

"Is it possible he was up to something? That you interrupted him?"

"What do you mean? Like burying a body?"

"I don't know. You said he was a stranger. What would a strange man be doing walking in the middle of nowhere in this town? Did you tell him your name?"

"No," Autumn said. Suddenly chilled, she wrapped her hands around her cup to warm them. "It all happened so fast. By the time I got back in my car and drove on, he was gone."

"That's so weird," Tana said. "I don't think you should go out there by yourself anymore."

Autumn scoffed. "I'll be fine. He was probably passing through."

Tana looked at her for a long moment, the unsaid truth in her dark eyes. No one ever "passed through" Pine Hollow. It was the sort of out-of-the-way burg that barely showed up on maps. With a population of a little over eight hundred people, it was a tight-knit little community where there was no such thing as a stranger.

"It's okay," Autumn said, forcing a note of dismissal into her voice. "I hate having run-ins with people like that. He brushed off my apology like I was being insincere."

"Fuck him," Tana said, waving a hand. "You don't owe him anything."

"Yeah," Autumn agreed, but she knew she'd be thinking about the mysterious man with the magnetic eyes all day.

***

Around noon, Autumn grabbed her earbuds and walked down Main Street to get lunch.

The clouds had parted somewhat creating little gaps for the sun to pour through in muted bands. Main Street was a perfect place to people-watch, especially during lunch hour.

Construction workers sat on a low stone wall outside the courthouse eating sub sandwiches and laughing over something only they could hear. Two young mothers walked with their babies in strollers window shopping as they sipped iced coffees. It was an idyllic picture of small-town life on a fall afternoon. But as with everything, the darkness lay just beneath like silt at the bottom of a sparkling lake. Autumn knew better than anyone what sort of terrors lurked in the shadows of an otherwise innocent façade.

She shoved her hands in the pockets of her coat and kept her head down, always wary of running into someone she knew. She'd managed to keep her distance from her father for ten years despite living in the same tiny community, but she was sure one day her luck would run out.

As she listened to Led Zeppelin's "No Quarter," she thought about the man with the dark eyes walking through the woods as if he owned them.

Inside Klinger's Deli, she ordered the usual for herself and Tana—two turkey sandwiches with the works, two massive chocolate chip cookies, and two peach iced teas—and leaned against the wall in a corner to wait, scrolling through her playlist to pass the time. After a few minutes, the hairs on the back of her neck prickled and she looked up, certain she was being watched.

The man in the flannel shirt stood at the counter, openly staring at her.

Adrenaline coursed through her veins, making her dizzy. What if Tana was right and she'd interrupted him in the middle of something unsavory? It wouldn't be hard for him to find out who she was, not if he were careful with his questions. The people of Pine Hollow were generally a trusting sort. Most of them still left their doors unlocked at night. There was no reason for fear or paranoia in a place where the crime rate was almost non-existant.

When the man moved toward her, she put her head down and studied her phone intently, hoping he was walking to the bathroom. Instead, he stopped directly in front of her. Drowned in his shadow, she had no choice but to look up.

Autumn was taller than average, around five eight, but he still towered over her. Those jet eyes met hers, but there was no animosity in them. Only curiosity.

She took out her earbuds out and attempted a little smile. "Hi."

"Hi," he said. His voice was deep and rich. "Taking a break from running people down?" His face was serious, but his eyes were smiling. She surprised herself by keeping her eyes level with his gaze, despite its intensity.

"It's exhausting," she said, playing along. "I need to keep my energy up. There's going to be a bunch of elderly people at a crosswalk later."

He laughed softly, a deep baritone rumble in his chest, and crossed his arms in front of him. "I'm Killian Quint, by the way."

"Autumn," she said, keeping her surname to herself. She stuck out her hand, expecting him to crush it in his massive palm, but he was gentle and his hand warm.

"I'm sorry about this morning," he said. "You caught me in a bad mood, and I shouldn't have taken it out on you."

"No, it's okay," she said. Any frustration she'd been carrying from their encounter had evaporated now that she was face-to-face with him. "I would have been irritated too if someone had nearly hit me."

"I should have been paying attention," he said, shaking his head.

"Did you move here recently?" she asked.

"Do I stick out like a sore thumb?"

"No," she said quickly. "I just... I know pretty much everyone in Pine Hollow."

"Ah," he said, looking past her for a moment. "Well, moved here recently, but I don't know for how long."

"You're here for work?"

"Sort of. One of those things that's temporary until I decide it's not, I guess."

"Autumn, your order's up," Daniel called from behind the counter, and she waved to show she'd heard him.

"Sorry, I'd better get back to work. My friend is waiting for her lunch," Autumn said.

"Ah, okay. Do you work around here?"

"Down the street."

"Well, I'd love a tour of the town from someone who knows it so well. If you're not too busy."

"What, today?" she asked, startled. *Is he asking me out?*

"Or tomorrow," he said with a little smile. "Whenever you're free. My schedule is flexible."

"I guess I could do it Thursday after work," she said haltingly.

Isn't it a bit foolhardy to be alone with a stranger? a voice whispered in her mind. Yet how was she supposed to meet someone nice if she didn't take a chance? She'd been saying no to possibilities for so long, doing it was what came naturally. The thought of telling him no created an ache in the pit of her stomach, a feeling so foreign she didn't recognize it for what it was: the fear of losing something she truly wanted.

Something in Killian gave her a good feeling. She felt they could be friends—or more.

"Sounds good. We could meet here?"

"Sure." She smiled. "Is six okay?"

"Perfect," Killian said, his return smile genuine. It lit up his face, transforming it from vaguely threatening to something beautiful.

She grabbed her order from the counter and hurried back to the office, already regretting telling him yes.

***

"Don't do it," Tana said around a mouthful of a turkey sandwich.

Autumn sighed and broke apart her cookie into manageable pieces. "I know what I said earlier, how I made him seem, but I swear, he was totally different. Not angry or hostile at all. There's something about him. I can't describe it. And wasn't it you demanding yesterday I meet guys, perhaps get laid eventually?"

Tana put down her sandwich and looked at Autumn incredulous. "You're gonna have sex with him?"

"No, of course not. I need to know someone well before that happens." She frowned. "I guess it's not a 'real' date. But maybe one day it could lead to *that*. Shit. Why did I tell him yes?" Autumn groaned, wrapping an arm around her stomach. "He's going to spend an hour with me and realize how fucked up I am and go running for the hills."

"You are *not* fucked up," Tana said firmly. "He'd be lucky to have you. I'm only saying, if you do this, be careful. Stay in public places and take the pepper spray I gave you. Be like Fox Mulder and trust no one."

Autumn laughed and pushed her hair back. "I feel like I'm losing my mind. What's wrong with me? If you'd told me a week ago I would be entertaining thoughts of going out with some strange, bearded giant, I would've laughed in your face."

It was true. She felt oddly giddy, her stomach a mass of nervous wires crossed with one another. How long had it been since she felt that way about a man? Six years? Eight? She'd lost count.

"I want to meet this guy," Tana said, watching Autumn carefully. "Any man who can get you wound up like this must be somethin'."

"Come with me to the deli tomorrow. You can meet him and give me an out if I change my mind."

"Okay, but if he turns out to be a psycho I'm gonna say *I told you so* every day for the next year."

"Deal."

***

That night, Autumn dreamt. It was the kind of dream that had her, rather than the other way around.

She sat in the backseat of a car as a skeletal bald man drove through a darkened city. The shushing of tires on wet blacktop was as calming as a lullaby, but she couldn't relax. The darkness was hungry. She scooted as far into the corner of the backseat as she could, wanting her mommy. She was seven years old and her mommy wasn't coming.

She looked down at the doll the man had given her and shuddered. Half the baby's flaxen hair was missing, winky eyes rolling back in her head, ugly as sin. Ugly as Autumn. The man had told her the doll was there to watch her. If you try to escape, he said, I'll know because the doll will know.

A phone burred near Autumn's ear and she jerked awake in the pre-dawn gloom. She looked around in panic, certain for a long moment the man had climbed out of her dream and sat on her bed. She surveyed the room warily. Everything seemed normal.

Huh. The bald man hadn't shown up in a dream for months. She was slipping. The nightmare disquieting. It happened when she didn't take care of herself. Sleep, fresh food, water: it wasn't so hard, but some days it was more challenging than others to focus on her needs. She was much more comfortable on the opposite side of things, taking care of others.

"Hello?" she murmured into the phone.

"Hey, it's me," Tana Jones said softly. Her voice was hoarse from lack of sleep. "Did I wake you?"

"Yeah, but I'm glad you did," Autumn said, running a hand through her long, chestnut hair.

"Bad dreams?"

"Always."

"Listen, I know it's early, but I just wanted to give you a heads up. Tommy Napier died early this morning."

Autumn closed her eyes against the news as a tortured knot formed in her belly. Tommy Napier was a vulgar, alcoholic asshole, but he was also the father of a little girl who desperately needed him. Brooke Napier was only seven years old and had already faced so many challenges in life.

"What happened?" she asked.

"Car crash on Route 9. It was right after the bars closed so I'm guessing alcohol was a factor, but Dave said the tox reports will take a little while."

Dave was Chief David Mulligan of the Pine Hollow Police Department, a man as kind and fair as they came. Autumn and Tana were always grateful for his help since his predecessor was on the far opposite end of the spectrum when it came to lending a hand to the Board of Social Workers.

"Has his family been notified?" Autumn asked heavily. The sun was barely up over the horizon and already she was tired of this day.

"Michael Napier was called to the morgue to identify him," Tana said, and Autumn cringed. Tommy's father was a mean-spirited old ghoul who took his pain out on other people. She could only imagine what this news would bring out in him.

"What about Rose?" she asked.

"Dave sent a deputy out to Tommy's house about an hour ago. Do you want me to meet you out there?"

Autumn smiled sadly. Tana had a million and one responsibilities of her own to attend to, but she was always willing to drop everything to help her best friend.

"No, that's okay," Autumn said. "I don't want Rose and Brooke to feel overwhelmed by too many people. Today will be hard enough for them as it is."

"Yeah," Tana agreed. "Well, if you change your mind, I'm only a phone call away."

Autumn thanked her and hung up, then lay back down for a moment and hugged her pillow for comfort. *Maybe I should get a cat*, she thought briefly, *something to love that can love me back*. It was a thought she entertained at least once a month, but she'd never go through with it. As much as she loved animals, she couldn't bear the thought of being responsible for another living thing. When she inevitably failed in her ability to take proper care of it, she knew she'd be devastated. Depression and anxiety stole so much.

A hot shower helped a little. She soaped up quickly and dressed in her typical uniform, a black t-shirt, dark jeans, and black boots. The hills of Pine Hollow carried rough terrain, so she needed to dress practically. She tied her hair up into a loose bun and left her glasses on, too tired to bother with contacts. Phone, charger, keys, and her favorite black military-style jacket, which was hooded and had lots of pockets. She hated carrying a purse.

The drive out to the Napier's was full of pearly tangerine light; a heavy fog had drifted through overnight and the sun appeared to be filtered through cotton. Fall was a beautiful time of year in Pine Hollow, with every tree aflame and the shifting skies reflecting shades of lapis lazuli and citrine. Autumn rolled down the window and stuck her hand out, allowing the wind to buffet her skin as she wound through the trees.

Brooke's home was a bungalow set among thick pines. The front yard was shaggy from all the recent rain, the driveway cluttered with three pickup trucks in various stages of repair. Tommy was—had been—a mechanic and was rarely without a project. Autumn maneuvered her Camry behind one of them and parked, sitting quietly for a moment. Her job was never easy, but some days were harder than others. Angry mothers had come for her with claws out, she'd had bottles thrown at her head, even a shotgun pulled on her, but none of them would compare to the look she was about to see on Brooke's face. It tore at her heart. She wrapped an arm around her stomach, wishing she'd thought to bring a roll of antacids along.

Rose was sitting on the covered front porch, wrapped in a blanket and smoking despite the oxygen tank that sat at her side when Autumn walked up. Autumn couldn't begrudge her a calming cigarette this time.

"Hey," Autumn said softly, stopping on the wooden steps. "I'm sorry to come by this early, but I heard the news, and I wanted to check on you guys. I'm so sorry, Rose."

At 33, Rose Napier was two years younger than Autumn but looked much older. Dark half-moons created shadows beneath her eyes. Her pale hair was pulled back and hidden under a kerchief. Rose's cancer was an aggressive type, already in the advanced stage. Before it took hold, she'd been a rare beauty who looked better without makeup, the kind of girl who loved to have a good time and threw her head back when she laughed. Autumn could never understand how she'd gotten mixed up with Tommy, a man who brushed against the seedy underbelly of bigger, neighboring towns daily. They'd been high school sweethearts, which must have counted for something.

His family was well-known and revered—or perhaps just feared—in Pine Hollow. Autumn pictured the Napier family estate, a sprawling white affair that overlooked the town, and imagined old Michael Napier sitting up there on a throne. He'd no doubt be looking down at his people in disdain, rolling around in the marrow of his grief, itching to take it out on someone.

"It's okay," Rose said, exhaling a stream of smoke through her nose. "Glad you're here."

Autumn stepped all the way up onto the porch and leaned against the railing. "How's Brooke?"

Rose looked out over the land, staying focused on middle-distance, and when she spoke her voice shivered just enough to tell Autumn all she needed to know.

"She went back to bed with her thumb in her mouth."

She's regressing, Autumn thought. A bad sign for a child who had been through as much as Brooke had. Physical abuse from her mother's former boyfriend, resulting in a brain injury. Severe anxiety, due in part to her parents' divorce and multiple attempts at reconciliation in an unstable home environment. Bullying from cruel kids at school who saw an easy target in a sensitive girl.

"May I?" Autumn asked, gesturing toward the screen door.

Rose nodded without turning her head and Autumn entered, catching the squeaky door before it could make a racket. She knew exactly where Brooke's bedroom was. She'd been there many times in the previous year for routine visits. The kitchen was redolent of warm buttery toast and cinnamon, comfort food for a fatherless child.

Autumn crossed the worn linoleum and stepped softly into Brooke's room, which smelled like baby shampoo. The lights were off, but beneath the blankets was a small lump, a fragile thing with blonde curls and earnest brown eyes that were closed against the world.

"Brooke?" Autumn said softly.

Brooke turned and peered at her over the comforter. "Hi."

"Can I come in?"

"You're already in."

Autumn sat on the edge of the bed and looked at Brooke's bookshelf, which contained a worn but well-loved collection of titles. A series of escapes, just like the ones Autumn had as a kid.

"I heard about what happened," Autumn said. "You feel like talking about it?"

"Not really," said Brooke, her voice muffled by the blankets.

"Okay, that's alright." Autumn waited for a few moments in silence.

"I didn't cry," Brooke said. Her thumb hovered near her mouth, wanting to go in, but she stopped it. "That's weird."

"It's not weird," Autumn said. "You're allowed to feel however you feel."

"Jessica Moore's grandpa died, and she cried for a week."

"Everyone reacts a little different when something like this happens," Autumn said, and a sudden memory popped into her head, unbidden: a graveyard, a cloudy sky, a murder of crows sitting on a fence like an omen. She'd been seven, the same age as Brooke. "There's no right or wrong way."

The little girl said nothing, but after a few minutes, her free hand crept out from beneath the blanket and reached for Autumn's. They sat in silence for a long while, hands intertwined, until Brooke fell into an uneasy sleep.

***

Back at their tiny office, Tana was waiting with hot coffee and donuts.

Autumn sat down at her desk without bothering to take her coat off. The morning chill had already seeped into her skin, along with the conversation she'd shared with Brooke and later, with Rose.

"You okay?" Tana asked quietly, pulling a chair to the opposite side of Autumn's desk to sit across from her.

Autumn nodded. "It's gonna be a rough few months."

"How is Rose?"

Tana had taken on the Napier case along with Autumn in the beginning, joining forces to provide a stronger front, and was well aware of the home situation. Tommy Napier was notoriously volatile, and it was customary for female social workers to double up when handling a tough job, at least until they could get a read on the situation. Social workers had some of the most dangerous jobs in the state. Showing up at a stranger's home to tell them they had to make changes to their lifestyle or parenting was often met with anger, resentment, suspicion, and, in a worst-case scenario, violence. Tommy—and his brothers, Bill and Austin—-had embodied all those and more in the past, and Tana knew full well how Autumn was feeling in that moment. Happy she'd never have to deal with his outbursts again, yet sad and worried for Brooke, and empathetic with Rose.

It was a no-win situation. Once cancer consumed her mother, Brooke's well-being would likely be transferred out of Autumn's hands. The girl would be referred to someone who specialized in child welfare. Worse, the Napier family would likely petition the court for custody of Brooke and given their influence in Pine Hollow, they'd win.

"Rose is scared," Autumn answered. "She's pragmatic, so all the worst futures for Brooke are going through her head right now. She doesn't want Tommy's family to get their hooks in her, but she'll have to designate someone as Brooke's caregiver in her will, and she has no family. The Napiers are it."

"Maybe this will be the best thing for her in the long run," Tana said gently. "The Napiers have enough money to give her anything she needs for the rest of her life."

"I hate the thought of her having to go through all this," Autumn said sadly, rubbing her forehead. "Leaving behind the only home she knows after losing both parents. And the not-knowing is the worst part. Not knowing when her mother is going to leave her, not knowing who will take care of her, not knowing if she'll even get to stay in Pine Hollow when all's said and done."

Tana reached across the desk and took her friend's hand. "Don't be mad."

Autumn looked up at her expectantly.

"I say this with all the love in the world, okay? I think you have allowed yourself to get too close to this case. You love Brooke because you have a big heart and because she's an awesome kid, but you may be also projecting some of your own stuff onto her. Don't you think so?"

Autumn looked closely at Tana, studied her fathomless onyx eyes, and remembered the images that had popped into her head just an hour earlier: the line of crows, memories of her

mother's funeral she'd kept pushed down for years. Yes, Brooke reminded Autumn of herself, and that was not a good thing.

"Yes," she said softly. "I guess I have been."

"You know I'm here for you, whatever you need. We'll get Brooke through this together, okay?"

"I can't ask for your help," Autumn said, shaking her head. "You have too much on your plate as it is."

"We're partners," Tana said stubbornly. "I'll figure it out."

Autumn sipped her coffee and smiled. "You're the best. Thanks, Tan."

"Just doing my best friend duty. Speaking of which, I don't like the sound of those dreams you were talking about earlier. What brought those on?"

"I don't know," Autumn said honestly. "I guess I could be taking better care of myself, but it feels bigger than that. I dreamed about the bald man again."

Tana's eyebrows went up. "He hasn't shown up in a while."

"I know. I was starting to think I was rid of him."

"You think you're working too hard? Maybe you need a mental health break. We could get out of town this weekend, head to Gatlinburg. You'll have to drive, though, so I can flash all the truck drivers on the way."

Autumn snorted laughter, grateful for the distraction. "You know it's cruel and unusual punishment to unleash those beauties on men when they'll never have a chance with you."

"What you call punishment, I call bestowing a gift," Tana said loftily and leaned back in her chair as she bit into a glazed donut. "Actually, a trip sounds damn good. Let's do it."

"Gatlinburg at this time of year is impossible unless you booked something back in May," Autumn said. "We'd have to sleep in the car. Besides, I have that *appointment* with Killian tomorrow night, remember? What if all goes well and he wants to meet up on the weekend?"

"He'll have to wait," Tana said, unfazed. "We could go to Nashville instead. Music City is full of hot and horny people, we'll get laid. Unless Killian does you..."

"Eh," Autumn said, her cheeks pinking. "I'm not in the mood for a weekend away." She sighed and slumped down further in her chair. "Maybe I'll become a nun."

"That's defeatist," Tana said.

"Well, what about you? What happened to Chloe?"

"She lives forty miles away, it was too much work."

Autumn laughed and shook her head. "You're a hypocrite."

"Am not. It's totally different. I've been putting myself out there for years. I'm not saying they've all been perfect, but they've been fun. Well, most of them."

Tana studied her for a moment, her expression serious. "You deserve to have someone love you, you know."

Autumn sat up in her chair and closed her jacket tight around her. "I know that."

"Don't get defensive. I'm trying to open your eyes."

"My eyes are wide open," Autumn said. "I know what I look like. I know how high maintenance I am. How many guys are there who could handle me at my worst? How many would put up with my night terrors or stick around long enough to see me through a depressive cycle, when I can barely find the energy to take a shower and wash my hair?"

Maybe this appointment with Killian is a bad idea after all. I should cancel.

"Autumn—"

"I know you mean well, and I love you for it," Autumn said, and swallowed hard. "I'm sorry, but you can argue with me all you want. I'm never going to see myself the way you do."

Tana shook her head, her lips pressed into a thin, tight line. "I hate your father."

"It's not all his fault."

"Don't you dare do that, don't you *dare*. It's 100% his fault. How many kids go through what you did? All the shit you saw..."

"I don't want to talk about him, okay? Not today."

Tana opened her mouth to say more, but Autumn was saved by the phone ringing. When Tana answered, Autumn took the opportunity to go to the bathroom, where the overhead fan was loud enough to drown out the sound of her crying.

Chapter Two

A thunderstorm unfurled above the town of Pine Hollow, rattling the windows in Autumn's bedroom, yanking her out of what was, for the first time in a while, a calm sleep.

She'd smelled the storm coming on the way home, wafting in through the windows of the car. Before she'd gone to bed, she'd left the curtains open to watch the lightning dance inside the gathering clouds. Storms had always been a comfort to her, particularly during the fall months. Nothing soothed her frazzled nerves the way dark skies and thunder did. Maybe that had been the catalyst for her uncharacteristically good rest, she thought and sat up in bed to watch the show outside.

She'd apologized to Tana before they left the office, not wanting to leave for the day with so much unsaid between them. Her friend had smiled and hugged her tightly.

"No sorries," Tana had said. "I'm sorry I got so deep on you. I only want to see you happy."

It was a truth that Autumn had known for years, since their college days, and she was afraid she'd never be able to express how grateful she was for Tana's veracity. Everyone in Autumn's childhood had seemingly made it their business to lie about things both big and small, leaving her in a perpetual state of distrust. Having someone like Tana in her life had helped to reset her inner compass.

Yes, Tana wanted to see Autumn settled, but Tana was at her most comfortable when she was with someone. She was an affectionate person who loved snuggling and would hug someone five minutes after meeting them. Autumn was the opposite. Closeness made her skin itch, and her palms sweaty. During the few brief relationships she'd had since college, sex was enjoyable, but afterward, she always felt anxious. She preferred to be alone because she'd never felt completely comfortable with another person, other than Tana. She'd never felt safe.

Again, she wondered why she'd been so quick to agree to go out with Killian. Something in him resonated with her, as it did with Tana. Autumn had learned to trust her instincts at a young age.

Her thoughts drifted back to Brooke, headed down the same path Autumn had taken. In that little girl, she saw her childhood fears playing out, the feelings of humiliation and worthlessness that took root and twined around her bones. Autumn hadn't had to face the added stress of losing both parents, as Brooke inevitably would. Being stripped of everything she'd known since birth might only pull her tighter into the cocoon of anxiety she often took refuge in. Perhaps Tana was right, though; Tommy's brothers and father certainly had enough money to give her the best of everything, even if they were not the best role models.

Yet blood didn't always bind people to the best caregiver. If the Napier family successfully petitioned the court for custody of Brooke, who knew what she might see and hear inside that big house on the hill? Autumn pictured destiny as a spoked wheel, guiding but never forcing, and each of those spokes had its own offshoots. There were so many directions the little girl's life could go in, the possibilities overwhelming to think about.

The storm cranked up further, lashing rain against the window as lightning painted stripes across the sky. Autumn lay back down and did something she hadn't done in years. She cast her mind outward, placing herself among the frenzied trees for a moment. When she was little it was the only way she could settle down for the night: to take herself out of her physical surroundings and, by extension, out of the anxiety she often felt after sunset. It wasn't a fear of the dark, but nervous anticipation of what she might hear coming from the other rooms in the house.

Autumn shoved the intrusive picture of her father from her mind and closed her eyes, focusing on the rain and wind. In moments, she was in a twilight sleep, walking through a hazy landscape she immediately recognized as Dream Country. There, her memories of Roland Phillips couldn't touch her.

***

The following day, as Autumn and Tara were ready to leave work, the phone rang.

"It's Rose," came the hoarse voice on the other end. Autumn's heart stuttered as her mind immediately went to the worst scenario: something was wrong. Brooke had run away, or worse. But Rose seemed calm, so Autumn forced herself to take a deep breath so she could focus.

"Hey," she said. "How are you feeling?"

"The same as always," Rose said. Autumn heard the squeak of a rocking chair and knew she was sitting on the front porch, smoking and watching the sun disappear behind the hills. "Tommy's funeral is set for Friday at one o'clock, Meadowview Cemetery. Brooke wants you to come."

Autumn shot a panicked look at Tana, who mouthed *What's going on?*

"I don't know, Rose, that might not be a good idea," she said, rubbing her forehead. "I'd like to pay my respects and everything, but I have to think about the best thing for Brooke. Having me there might complicate things with your family."

"I wouldn't ask, but she's not been herself, Autumn. It's scaring me. She has trouble sleeping, and when she does rest it takes everything I have to wake her up. I went into her room this morning to get her ready for school, and she wasn't moving. I thought…" She trailed off, and Autumn knew exactly what had gone through Rose's mind. "It took forever to get her going, more than usual. She was late for class."

"Do you want me to call Dr. Forrester in the morning? Make her an appointment?"

"She doesn't need a doctor," Rose said irritably. "She needs her daddy back."

Autumn closed her eyes and felt a tremor pass through her as a sudden memory flew up behind her eyes: her father coming into her bedroom with a gun in the middle of the night. He'd sat in the chair across from her bed and laid the gun across his lap. She'd watched through eyes narrowed to slits, pretending to be out. Eventually, she'd fallen asleep waiting for him to leave.

"Listen, as far as my family is concerned, you've done nothin' but help Brooke," Rose was saying. "You don't have to worry about them startin' any trouble. They wouldn't do that at Tommy's funeral."

"What about his family?" Autumn asked quietly.

"No one is going to mess with you," Rose said, her voice firm. "Brooke wants you there; so I want you there. Ain't no one gonna fuck with me on the day I bury my husband."

Autumn rolled her eyes up to the ceiling, wishing the heaviness in her chest would go away. "Okay. I'll come. Tell Brooke I'll be there."

"Thanks, girl. Friday at one."

Autumn hung up and looked at Tana, who was eyeing her warily.

"You'll be where?" she asked.

"Tommy's funeral," said Autumn, wincing.

"You are yankin' me."

"Afraid not."

Tana shook her head. "That is some dangerous shit, right there. First you accept a date with some strange guy and now you're walking into a family event full of people who hate us? You got a death wish?"

"They don't *all* hate us," Autumn said weakly.

"Tommy's family has had it out for both of us since day one," Tana argued. "The Napiers don't want anyone poking around in their business. Social workers are like their sworn enemies."

Autumn sighed heavily and wrapped her cross-body bag around herself. "I need to do it for Brooke. Maybe if they see that I'm there for her, they'll understand where I'm coming from a little more."

Tana gave her a look. They both knew better than that.

"Well...don't draw attention to yourself, okay? Stand in the back and duck out early. Keep your keys between your fingers when you walk out to the parking lot."

"It'll be broad daylight at the cemetery, I don't think they're going to jump me on the way to my car," Autumn said, exasperated at Tana's mothering.

"You can never be too careful with those people," Tana muttered as she locked the door behind them.

Chapter Three

The nerve-wracking 'Appointment with Killian' day dragged itself along like a dog with a broken leg. Autumn found herself looking at the clock much more often than she liked, and what was worse, Tana noticed it, too.

"You know what they say about a watched pot?" Tana said finally at three o'clock.

"I can't help it," Autumn said, running her fingers through her hair. "I feel like I'm going crazy. I've reread this email three times, and I still have no idea what it says."

"Time won't go any faster if you get yourself all worked up," Tana said.

"I know," Autumn sighed. "God, I'm a sad little person."

"You are not. Why would you say that?"

Autumn shrugged. "I feel like this is something normal people do every day. Go out on dates, meet new people, and it's not a big deal to them. Not that this is even a proper date, not really," she hastened to add. " But it's the closest thing I've had to one in a long time."

"It is a big deal," Tana said. "It takes a lot of courage to put yourself out there. Even if it's not a 'real' date to you, it's awesome you're opening yourself up a little."

"Thanks," Autumn said, and felt a rush of heat in her cheeks at the compliment. "I'm sorry, I know it's all I've talked about today. Tell me what's going on with you."

Tana shrugged. "Nothing, really. I think I want to take a break from dating. Just have some alone time with my cat, eat cold pasta at 2 a.m., and watch Netflix in my underwear."

"That sounds like the life," Autumn said. "Can I come, too?"

"Only if you don't bitch about what a messy little strumpet I am," Tana said with a laugh. "That was my beef with Chloe. She was some kind of neat freak. So annoying."

"You know I'm as messy as you are," Autumn said. "It's a wonder we've managed to keep the office so clean."

"It's only out of necessity. We'd be up shit creek without a paddle if things got disorganized around here."

Messes. Disorganization. Two things Autumn's father would never tolerate when she was younger. She suspected it was a large part of the reason why she allowed clutter to pile up in her home as an adult, why she left dirty dishes in the sink for longer than a day or two. Because she could.

It was a week for remembrances, and she was sick of them. Autumn pushed back her chair and stood so suddenly she felt blood rush to her feet.

"I'm gonna make some tea, do you want some?"

Tana waved a hand at her, deep into an email. "Nah, I'm good."

In the office's small kitchenette, Autumn sat at the table while she waited for the water to heat up and tried, unsuccessfully, to push thoughts of her parents from her mind. She remembered another kitchen in a different decade, a room flooded with seven a.m. sunlight.

Bacon smells and cartoon sounds, so it must have been a Saturday. Her mother stood at the stove in a cloud of freshly-brewed coffee, placing biscuits on a pan, then fluttered over to the sink to clean up.

Autumn would watch her mom and wonder when she'd break. To her 6-year old self, her mom seemed so fragile, like the skeleton of a tiny bird, ready to snap under the slightest pressure. Autumn always felt so sure she could fix her. Her young mind was filled with missives from educators and after-school-specials, telling her she was strong enough to resist drugs, to stand up for herself, to be of help to someone who needed it. But when the time came, she was never able to do any of those things. She was a fraud in a Pac-Man t-shirt.

Her father's presence in the room was oppressive. As always, she felt nervous, the sort of loose-bowels anxious that might precede a math test or the first step on a frozen pond.

He walked past her without acknowledgment, and she breathed relief onto her plate. He was a man of few words and less affection. Autumn couldn't recall him ever kissing her mother or putting his arm around her. As usual, her mom stood over the sink and busied herself so she wouldn't have to look the storm in the eye. Autumn could smell it building already, over the scent of his shaving cream and the tang of orange juice. Some days he simply woke up ready to fight.

Her dad plucked a mug from the drainer and filled it with coffee, his large, freckled hands efficient.

When did he become so mean? Why is he like this? Was it growing up poor? Never feeling good enough? Autumn sensed these inadequacies in herself, a great wave ready to crash. She was ugly and awkward, a fair student but truly good at almost nothing. Inadequacy bred ill-temper.

Autumn's father lunged for the sink, pushing her mom out of the way, and spat out his first drink of coffee. He wiped his mouth, then turned on the tap and drank directly from it, swishing it around before spewing it back into the basin.

"What the fuck is wrong with you?" he shouted. "You can't even rinse all the soap out of a goddamn coffee mug?"

Her mother's eyes were huge. Autumn blinked, and then he was on her mother, his big fist tangled in her hair. He held her over the sink and threw the offending mug into the soapy water. It must have hurt, and yet her mother never made a sound. Not even when he hit her with a closed fist in the small of her back. A kidney shot.

Back in the present, Autumn winced. *She was stronger than I knew.* As a kid, she'd confused silence with weakness, but her mother was just trying to survive. It was what her entire life had been about, and she'd kept winning the battle, but what did that victory earn her? A life lived in constant fear and pain until cancer finally took over.

For a long, intense moment, Autumn seriously considered abandoning her time with Killian in favor of driving to the liquor store. Instead, she got up and slid their seldom-used coffee maker into the trash.

***

At 5:45, Autumn logged off her computer and went into the bathroom to change from business casual to her favorite worn black jeans and a grey long-sleeved t-shirt. She left her hair down and went easy on the makeup, applying a little mascara and a rosy lip tint that tasted like

cherries.

"You ready?" Tana asked when she emerged, and Autumn knew what her friend was really asking. This was about more than a date.

"Yes," she said and drew a shaky breath. "I'm ready."

When they left the office, the sun was already lowering itself toward the horizon like a lady into a bathtub. Its rays cast a tangerine glow across Main Street. Autumn studied the purple shadows around them and thought about all the ways the night could end. It would certainly take the pressure off if she kept the idea in mind that Killian probably had no interest in her.

The warm glow of lights from the deli's windows beckoned them forward. Tana put her hand on Autumn's elbow to slow her down a bit.

"Remember what I said about staying in public places," she said. "And call me when you get home."

"I will," Autumn said with a little laugh. "You're making me nervous."

"I don't want you to be nervous. I want you to have a good time. But I also want you to keep your eyes open. Anything seems off, you get out. Don't worry about what he'll think. That's always a problem women have when it's time to defend themselves or run away—they're afraid of being seen as "crazy" or "dramatic". I learned that in my self-defense class."

"I think most people already think I'm crazy and dramatic," Autumn said, shooting a grin at Tana as she pulled open the door to the deli.

She'd been afraid Killian would be late, or worse, he wouldn't show, but he was already sitting in a booth near the front of the small space. He smiled and stood when he saw them, holding out a hand to Tana.

"Hi, I'm Killian," he said. That deep voice. Autumn was sure she'd be dreaming about it later.

"Hello," Tana said, looking up at him in frank awe. "Wow, you look like you could uproot a tree with your bare hands." She held out a hand. "I'm Tana Jones, Autumn's best friend."

He chuckled. "Nice to meet you. Thanks for the compliment—I think. Do you two work together?"

"We do," Autumn said, meeting his inky eyes. Something in them made her want to tell him every truth she had ever known. "She wanted to meet you before we left."

Tana shot her a look, but Killian only laughed.

"I understand," he told Tana. "Giant strangers don't exactly inspire confidence. Do you want to give me your phone number? I'll text you from mine, so you'll have it."

Tana smiled, and Autumn knew he'd scored big points with that one. "That's a good idea."

They exchanged info and Tana left after lifting an eyebrow at Autumn, which meant: *Have a good time, and I want to hear all about it later.*

"Any idea of where you want to go?" she asked Killian as they stepped outside.

"Well, I don't know anything about Pine Hollow, so that's up to you. Any landmarks or popular restaurants I should know about?"

The evening smelled like burning leaves and she breathed in deep, watching the horizon turn burnt orange against a velvety blue sky.

"I can think of some places," she said. "I was going to drive, but do you feel up to a walk? It's such a nice night."

They started walking east, toward the end of Main Street that backed up against a copse of trees. Autumn kept her hands in her coat pockets so she could open and close her fists periodically. It helped with the anxiety, which she was interested to note didn't so much relate to being alone with a stranger, but rather the idea he'd think she was boring.

"So what do you do?" she asked as they walked.

"I'm a freelance architect. I mostly worked for big firms back in Seattle, where I grew up, but it was only something to pay the bills. I prefer to do smaller jobs these days. They're more interesting."

"Wow. That sounds super impressive. Especially compared to what I do for a living," Autumn laughed.

"I'm sure that's not true," Killian said, smiling kindly at her. "What line of work are you in?"

"I'm a lowly social worker."

"Are you kidding? *That's* an impressive job, and a damn hard one. There's only so much learning you can do from books because a lot of it is intuition and emotional response."

"That's true," she said.

"Plus it's one of the most dangerous jobs in the country, especially for a woman."

She looked up at him in surprise. "You sound like you know a lot about it."

"My mother used to work with Child Protective Services," said Killian. "She had some horror stories. Honestly, it's pretty incredible that anyone would go into that line of work. You must be a very selfless person."

Autumn shrugged. "I don't know about that. I've always wanted to help people. My childhood was...pretty dark. Intense. I feel better if I'm doing some good for someone else."

She felt his gaze on her as they made it to the end of Main and crossed into Lykins Park. He seemed to be looking for the right words.

"That just shows what a good person you are," he said finally. "People with difficult childhoods often become difficult adults. The fact that you went the opposite way with your life says a lot."

"I try to make every day worth something," she said. She felt heat rising up her neck and quickly changed the subject, deeply uncomfortable with the spotlight. "So why did you come to Pine Hollow? It's not exactly a thriving spot for architecture."

"It's...complicated," he said.

They slowed down and sat on a nearby bench watching the night unfurl around them. Autumn turned toward him and realized how warm he was. Heat radiated from his body like a furnace. It was incredibly comforting, and she forced herself to keep a demure distance, secretly wishing she could lean into him.

"I'm sorry. I didn't mean to pry," she said.

"No, no, it's not that," he said. "I'm not sure where to start. I guess it would be with my good friend Amy."

Amy? Autumn's stomach clenched into a fist. So he had a girlfriend after all. The pain was surprising, considering how little she knew about this man.

"She married another good friend of mine, Brian, and they passed through Kentucky on their honeymoon a few months ago," he went on, and Autumn's relief was almost tangible. "Brian said they drove through a place called Pine Hollow, and he made it seem like this perfect little Appalachian jewel no one knew about. The more they talked it up, the more I wanted to come here."

"So you came here on a whim?" she asked. It was the kind of impulsive act she'd always wished she were capable of but would never be able to pull off due to her anxiety.

"I've been wanting to get away from the West Coast for a while now. I still love it, always will, but I needed a change. I thought I'd come here, check it out for myself, and if it grows on me, I might build a house here. There are plenty of job opportunities around here, between the horse breeders and the university in Leitchfield."

He has to stay, Autumn suddenly thought, and clenched her fists inside her pockets. "Well, what do you think so far?"

He met her gaze, the smile on his lips faltering before it reached his eyes. "I think I like Pine Hollow quite a bit."

They sat in comfortable silence for a moment. Autumn studied him from the corner of her eye, noting the blue work shirt he wore with the sleeves rolled up to expose his massive forearms. No coat, even though Autumn could see her breath since the sun had disappeared. Inside the holler, fall evenings were much colder than they were anywhere else.

"So where are we?" he asked softly, watching her.

"This is Lykins Park," she answered. "No playground—that's on the other side of town, at Lantern Hills—so it's a good place to come when you want to sit and read or have lunch. No noisy kids to interrupt. If you want a good place for lunch, you have to try Gertie's on Maple Avenue. It's a tiny little blue house that's been converted to a diner. Gertie Mac and her husband Joe opened it up back in the '70s, but she runs it by herself since he died. The best fried chicken you'll ever find."

She turned to smile at him and was startled to discover he'd leaned closer to her when she wasn't paying attention; their faces were just inches apart. Autumn took a breath and searched his eyes briefly, looking for any sign of danger, but he was calm.

"I'm sorry, am I crowding you?" he asked, pulling back. "You seemed cold."

"I did?" she breathed. She realized she was shivering, but she wasn't sure if it was from the cold or nerves. His eyes reflected moonlight like a dark ocean.

"Why don't you let me walk you back to your car?" he said. "You should get warm, or you'll be sick."

"No," she said quickly. "I mean, I haven't shown you anything yet. I'm fine."

He gave her a little smile and ducked his head for a moment. "Alright. But maybe we should start walking again. Sitting here on this cold bench isn't going to warm you up."

"I know where we can go," she said, relieved he wasn't going to insist on ending the night early.

She led him through the trees, weaving expertly between branches even when the moon was shadowed by clouds. They were on a path she'd taken many times over the years, one used mostly by kids who wanted a shortcut to the swimming hole. As they walked, the conversation turned to favorite movies, books, and music. Autumn was delighted to find an avid reader in him, and he seemed especially pleased to discover she had more than a passing knowledge of metal and old country songs. Some of his favorite tunes were ones she often sang in the shower, although she'd never tell him that.

After several minutes, they emerged in a clearing lit by the orange sodium lights placed around the edge of the falls for safety.

"The quarry," she said, turning back to look at Killian. "Where every Pine Hollow kid has learned to swim since at least 1950."

"It's beautiful," he said, his voice so earnest she wondered for a moment if a hurtful memory had been jogged. "I didn't think places like this existed outside of the Pacific Northwest."

The setting was gorgeous. Surrounded by pines, the rocks they stood on towered over the water by fifty feet or so. Only the bravest kids ever jumped, or the ones who had nothing to lose. Autumn had jumped hundreds of times.

"There's never anyone out here this time of year, but in summer half the town comes out during the day," she said. "There's a little road down there. See it winding through the trees? It's accessed from Maple Street. If you know where to look, it'll take you to a tree with a tire swing on it. The cops gave up on trying to keep people from swimming...nothing else for kids to do in this town...so every year they replace the rope on the swing and make safety sweeps on hot days."

"What about criminal activity?" Killian asked suddenly, his gaze searching the tree line. "Anything ever happen out here?"

Autumn shrugged, caught off guard. "Not that I know of, other than petty stuff. People fighting, that sort of thing. Pine Hollow is pretty tame for the most part. Drugs are always an issue, but that's any town."

He turned to her, shoulders tensed. His breathing became sharper, as though he was trying to catch a specific scent. "Are there houses out here?"

"A mile or so down, maybe, where the lake feeds into the Kentucky River. Why?"

"Just wondered about who owns all this," he said, giving her a tight smile. "I'd love to build out here."

Autumn's heart rate sped up. She had good instincts, and they were telling her something wasn't right. She still didn't feel he was dangerous, but she didn't want to press him about what was really going on. She felt, with absolute certainty, that Killian was being untruthful.

And a big part of her wanted to know why.

***

As soon as they left the clearing, Killian seemed to slip into a more relaxed mood. Autumn sensed he'd been deeply uncomfortable about something, but she was loath to try and get it out of him. If he wanted her to know, he'd tell her.

Encouraged by his gentle smile, she showed him the bandstand, the courthouse with its original keystone from 1887, and the old jail. Something told her he'd appreciate the ancient buildings, with their weight of history and callbacks to another time, and she was right. He pointed out details in the arched windows she'd never noticed and expressed an interest in the town's only Catholic church, St. Mary's. Stained glass windows threw bright jewels of color onto the sidewalk like an invitation.

"Do you practice? A religion, I mean?" she asked, then immediately regretted it. "I'm sorry if that's intrusive..."

"No, it's not at all," he said with a smile. "I used to. My parents raised me Catholic, and we went to church every Sunday, but it always just felt like something I had to do. I haven't been in years, but I still love the buildings themselves. The older ones, at least, they're beautiful. How about you?"

Autumn shook her head. "I've always been interested in studying different religions, but I don't practice. It's just not for me."

"Must have been hard, growing up in a small town and not going to church."

He wasn't judging, simply making an observation. A correct one.

"Yeah, I'm kind of the black sheep of Pine Hollow," she said with a little laugh. "Not an outcast, because everyone knows me, and they're friendly enough. More like the weirdo goth cousin the family doesn't understand."

She kept her tone light and thought he might laugh along with her, but his eyes were serious when she turned to look at him.

"I'm sorry you feel that way," he said. "I know that feeling. It's not fun."

"You do?" she asked, surprised. "I would never have imagined you ever felt like an outsider."

"People see me, this big guy who usually has a scowl on his face, and think they have me pegged in under a minute. I'm some asshole lumberjack with about two brain cells to spare, or I'm a meathead who uses his fists all the time. I love the woods, and I've split my share of logs, but that's as far as those comparisons go. When I was younger, it was worse. I was good at sports, so to everyone in my town that was all I could do."

"I pity anyone who never took the time to get to know you." The words were out of her mouth before she even realized she was going to say them out loud, and a familiar heat rose to her chest and neck. She'd given away too much.

But he didn't laugh, and he didn't look away in embarrassment. Instead, he studied her face as if she was the most beautiful thing he'd ever seen.

Several seconds went by. Autumn felt her stomach twist in anticipation; was he going to kiss her? Touch her face? She felt weak-kneed at the thought of either and wished desperately for something, anything, to happen. But he stood completely still, his dark hair painted red and blue in the light thrown from the stained glass window above.

"It's getting late," she said finally with a nervous little laugh. "I should let you go." He looked pained for a moment, and then it was gone, like a cloud passing over the sun.

"Sure, I should probably try to get some rest. The time change is kind of killing me."

"Oh, man, I bet. Where are you staying? Someplace with a good bed, I hope?"

She realized too late how provocative that sounded and felt her cheeks color, but Killian didn't indicate he'd read anything inappropriate in it.

"Pine Hollow B&B," he answered. "The bed is pretty good, although it could be bigger. It's hard for me to find one that fits."

Autumn's thoughts went to dimly lit places where Killian dominated a four-poster and growled gently against her ear. Her face nearly ignited at the force of her thoughts, and she cleared her throat to push her focus back to the present.

"Well, my car is parked right over there."

"I'll walk you," he said.

She leaned against the car and looked up at him. He was backlit by the moon, broad shoulders painted celestial blue. His face was in shadow, but she could feel his gaze on her and wondered if he could sense how badly she wanted him to kiss her.

"Thank you so much for the tour," he said softly.

"You're very welcome; it was my pleasure. Did you walk here?" The B&B was just a few streets over. "I can give you a ride back."

"No, that's okay. Thank you for the offer. I like walking on nights like this."

"It is pretty nice," she agreed. "The moon is beautiful."

He turned to look up at it. "It'll be full in a few days."

"The Harvest Moon," Autumn said.

"That's right," he said, turning back to her. "The equinox will come soon after."

"The equinox is when there's an equal amount of day and night, right?"

"Yes. The official start of fall."

There was something in his voice, a slight change that Autumn couldn't measure. Not sadness, not anger, but...an edge. Maybe he was feeling uncertain about his future and whether he should go back to Seattle.

"My favorite time of year," she said lightly. "The trees change, the relentless summer heat goes away for good, and we get Halloween. Which should be a national holiday, honestly."

"You love Halloween," he said. It wasn't a question, but a musing that came with a smile.

"Sure," she said. "Pumpkins and ghosts and candy. Scary movies. Plus the town looks gorgeous around that time because the Public Works Department decorates Main Street with twinkle lights and mums in hanging baskets."

She was grasping at anything to make Pine Hollow seem like an appealing place to live, she realized, and that scared her. Autumn had never been one to rely on someone else for her happiness, had never been inclined to need another person so completely everything else was blotted out. It was a frightening precursor to losing oneself, she imagined, and she'd fought hard for her autonomy.

Killian suddenly stepped closer to her, leaving a bare few inches of space between them. Autumn flinched instinctively, and he noticed. Slowing his movements, he brought his hands up and cradled her face with extreme care, tilting it up toward his.

"This is going to sound like the worst kind of line," he said, his voice a rough whisper, "But you look incredibly beautiful in the moonlight."

Autumn swallowed hard and shook her head. For some reason, his choice of words made her feel like crying. Maybe because her father had been on her mind lately, the man who had called her Ugly Duckling for most of her childhood.

"That's very kind," she said, fighting hard to keep the tears out of her voice. "But you don't have to say that."

The scowl on his face might have scared her at any other time, but there, beneath the moon, with his warm fingertips so gently skimming her jaw, she only felt sorry she couldn't believe him.

"I know I don't," he said. "You're not...You're an interesting person, Autumn. I'm glad to know you."

I'm glad to know you too, she wanted to say, but she couldn't bring the words out. Something was happening; her limbs were heavy with desire, her face tingled where he touched her, and all she could think about was the way he'd taste when he finally brought his mouth to hers.

But he didn't kiss her. Instead, he turned abruptly and walked toward Maple Street, hands shoved into his pockets so that his shoulders were hunched up.

Autumn sagged against her car on legs that trembled like leaves in the wind. It was a full minute before she could find the strength to climb into the driver's seat.

Chapter Four

When Autumn got home, she checked her phone and saw two missed text messages from Tana.

Are you home yet? I am dyyiinnnnggg, he's so hot! Please tell me you did it.

Call me the second you get in. THE SECOND.

Autumn smiled and dialed Tana's number; she answered before the first ring ended.

"First off, tell me you're okay."

"I'm fine," Autumn said with a laugh.

"How was it? Where did you go? Did he make a move? Is he your boyfriend?"

"It was very nice, and no, he didn't make a move. Well, kind of, at the end. But not really."

"Uhhhh, you're killing me," Tana said impatiently.

"Well, I showed him around town, took him to the quarry..."

"I told you to stay in public places."

"...And when we said goodnight he put his hands on my face, super gently, like he was going to kiss me. But I guess he changed his mind at the last second."

"Oh." Tana sounded deflated. "Well, did you have a good time? What's his story, anyway?"

"He's from Seattle. Get this—he's an architect. The guy's majorly smart. Loves his mom, I could tell by the way he talked about her. She worked with CPS for years, so he knows all about what we do every day. He said he's thinking of moving here, but he wants to scout things out first. He listens to Baroness and his favorite movie is *The Shining*."

"Autumn. He's your soulmate."

"I don't know about that," Autumn mused. "I like him, though. I like him a lot."

"Did he ask you out again?"

Autumn frowned. "No. He didn't give me his number, either. But he told me he's staying at the B&B."

"I got a good feeling from him. You know how I am with people, I get a vibe," Tana said.

Autumn wanted desperately to believe Killian was a good guy, but he was still largely a mystery. There were moments during their evening when his mood had shifted and it was unsettling. Reading people to accurately predict their reactions was something she was trained to do, and she was good at it, but there were so many things about him she couldn't read.

"How was your night?" Autumn asked.

"Laid back. Pizza, snuggles with Chonk, a tawdry paperback, and a glass of wine. I'm living my best life."

Autumn kicked off her boots and slung her coat and bag into a chair. "Sounds heavenly. What's the book?"

"It's called *Just After Dusk*," Tana said. "I mostly just read the dirty parts."

"Sinner."

"You know I am."

Autumn laughed. "I'll see you in the morning."

"Not if I see you first," Tana said.

It was a quote from one of Autumn's favorite movies, *Stand By Me*, and for some reason it made her feel like crying. She swallowed hard and looked at her reflection in the window: a pale, fragile girl stared back.

"You're a really good friend, you know that?" she said suddenly. "I don't think I say it often enough."

"Well, thank you, babe," Tana said, clearly touched.

"I mean it. You're always taking care of me and making sure I'm okay. Sometimes all the anxiety pulls me inside my head so much that I don't realize I'm coming across as selfish. I think...I think all the shit I'm dealing with mentally can make me a bad friend."

"You are the least selfish person I know," Tana said. The quiet strength in her voice told Autumn how sincere she was. "You don't have to explain anything to me, honey. I know you better than anyone. And you are as good a friend to me as I try to be to you."

After they hung up, Autumn ran a hot bath and shuddered into the steam, lying back against the tub with her eyes closed. Some days were worse than others for her insecurities, but if she concentrated on something hard enough she could usually fight them off. When an image of Killian popped into her head, she smiled and sank further into the water, remembering the feel of

his hands on her face and the look in his eyes as they stood within the stained-glass glow of the church. He'd left so abruptly, but all the signs of attraction were there.

She wondered whether he was a good kisser and suddenly got an image of those devastating eyes looking up at her from between her legs. The thought jolted her and she shivered despite the heat of the water, imagining the feel of his rough beard on the soft skin of her inner thighs. His big hands cradling her bottom as he drank from her like a man slaking thirst, her fingers winding into his hair to hold him there.

Autumn's hand moved through the steam to find herself slick and ready. It didn't take long. The memory of his gaze and the heat of his body as they sat together on the bench was enough to send her out of control. She moaned and bit her lip, legs trembling beneath the surface of the water as she coasted down. It'd been so long since she'd wanted someone so badly that she barely recognized this desire.

As her breathing slowed, Autumn settled comfortably and relaxed, her thoughts still firmly on Killian. In moments, she was asleep in the water, and her dreams were strange, shifting things.

She was in Dream Country, the place her mind retreated to when she allowed herself to push past her physical surroundings. Pine trees streamed past as she ran through the dense forests of Pine Hollow, familiar guardians pointing the way with swaying branches. She'd come here many times since childhood. It was a safe refuge, one she immediately recognized as a dream. In this lucid state, she felt as conscious as she did during waking hours but safer.

Killian was beside her, running swiftly and with no regard to the cold despite his nakedness. He seemed not to notice her, keeping his head down as he navigated the trees seemingly without even looking at them. When she looked up, a full moon shone down over the town—a bloated silver ball hovering in the darkness. Suddenly Autumn was afraid.

"Killian," she called, but the wind made her voice insubstantial. "Killian, slow down."

But he kept up his pace as the air seemed to vibrate around him. It was only when they reached the edge of the forest he slowed. Autumn followed him to the edge of the quarry. She looked down at the surface of the water, where the moon reflected shards of silver and blue and saw her image there as well. Pale and transparent, with only darkness where her eyes should be. A specter.

She sucked in a ragged breath and turned to Killian, needing to find something solid to assure herself she was okay, but he was paying no attention to her.

He stood with his feet planted in the dirt, blood streaming down his chin and bare chest in ribbons, and lifted his face to the moon in a primal scream.

Autumn jerked awake, flailing in the tub as she pulled herself back to consciousness and gasping for breath. Her lungs burned, her body was chilled.

In her mind played the haunting strains of an old Lead Belly song.

Tell me where did you sleep last night? In the pines, in the pines, where the sun don't ever shine. I would shiver the whole night through.

***

When her alarm went off at seven, Autumn woke slowly.

Her limbs felt oddly heavy, as though she'd been drugged and her mind was wrapped in fog. She recalled her dream and frowned, rubbing her eyes with the heels of her hands. Such a strange one, even for her. The vision of Killian covered in blood made her shudder as she sat up and kicked off the blankets.

A hot shower helped, although the tub reminded her of the *other* thoughts she'd entertained the previous night. She smiled as she washed her hair, knowing it was not going to be a day for glasses and no makeup. If Killian came looking for her, he was going to find the best possible version.

She stopped for coffees on the way to the office and added a double shot of espresso to hers. She'd need it to get through the day.

Tana was already there filing paperwork when Autumn walked in. She accepted her coffee gratefully before filling Autumn in on the day's workload.

"Mrs. Crawford is being moved to a senior care facility," she said. "Her daughter finally showed up from Florida and agreed to foot the bill."

"Well that's some good news," Autumn said. Mrs. Crawford had been declining in both physical and mental health for years but had no family nearby to help her out. Autumn had met her daughter, Lacy, during her brief visit the year before. She'd found her to be extremely self-involved and out of touch with her mother's needs.

"Yeah, but I doubt she'll be there long," Tana said sadly. "Most seniors who move to long-term care facilities don't last."

Autumn pondered that as she sipped her coffee, wincing at the bitter aftertaste. She had to take it slow, otherwise, she'd be climbing the walls by lunchtime.

"I'll drive out there today and help her get settled in," she said.

"I'm sure she'd appreciate it. Oh, and the unemployment system is down again, so brace yourself for the calls. I've already taken three, and it's not even eight-thirty yet."

"Shit," Autumn mumbled. "Why can't the state hire someone to update their site? Hell, I'll do it for free. I took a semester of coding and design."

The morning flew by in a blur, with both of them fielding calls and attempting to get their schedules in order. When Chief David Mulligan walked in, Autumn was shocked to see it was already noon. She'd been so swamped she hadn't even stopped for a bathroom break.

"Hey, Chief," Tana said. "I hope you've got some good news for us because we could sure use it."

"Sorry, I'm all out of good news," David said. "I just wanted to stop by and see how y'all are gettin' along."

Tana shot a look at Autumn. Chief never stopped by without a reason.

"We're fine," Autumn said. "Everything okay?"

He squinted at her, a surefire sign he was about to say something he knew she wouldn't like. Autumn put down the stack of papers in her hand and gave him her full attention.

"Rose Napier said she asked you to go to Tommy's funeral," he said gently. "I don't know if it's a good idea."

"I know, I told her the same thing," Autumn said. "But she thinks it'll help Brooke."

"Austin and Bill Napier aren't men you want to mess with. We'll have a presence at the cemetery because Rose asked us to be there, but if they get riled up and cause a scene and we have to haul them outta there, it's not gonna be good for anybody."

Autumn felt a flare of anger ignite in her belly. Never mind that these were things she'd already thought about. Never mind her main concern was a little girl who stood to lose everything. It burned that she had to tiptoe around these two men because of the perceived power they held in their small town.

David had tried for years to pin them down, to make anything stick, but they were slippery fish. The Napier family went back generations inside their huge house on the biggest hill, and there were whispers in the valley about their involvement in the drug trade. Tommy, Austin, and Bill had seen their fair share of trouble over the years, but their last name had helped them avoid any lasting retribution. Their father, Michael, made sure their noses were clean no matter how many brushes they had with the law. Tommy had the longest rap sheet, a string of arrests stemming from marijuana possession, and a handful of DUIs in his 20's, but all three Napier boys had brushed up against the darkness in Pine Hollow at some point: bar fights, domestic disputes, trespassing.

Autumn had often wondered why they didn't keep a lower profile, but all it came down to was a simple truth: they didn't care. Growing up with money and influence had left them untouchable, at least in their minds.

Like any family of means with secrets to keep, the Napiers despised the idea of a stranger coming into their circle and butting in. From day one, Tommy and his brothers had made Autumn's job ten times harder by refusing to cooperate with her. It wasn't uncommon for Tommy to sabotage home visits by having Bill stop by with his dogs—two Great Danes built like horses—to get Brooke too excited to sit still and talk.

"I'm not going to the church, that feels too private," Autumn said, trying hard to keep the anger out of her voice. David was only trying to help, as ham-handed as it came across. "But I don't see the harm in going to the cemetery to show Brooke that I'm still here for her."

David nodded. He looked tired, more so than Autumn had ever seen him.

"Alright, but I want you to let me know when you get there," he said. "Them boys have already got drunk, wrecked Rooster's bar, and broke a bunch of stuff the day they found out about Tommy. They're liable to show their asses again when they have to face buryin' him."

Rooster was an old friend of her dad's, the only one she had ever liked. He was a lean and rangy sixty-five, a dyed-in-the-wool biker who still wore a leather vest every day. Not known for taking any shit, especially in his bar. *He must've handed the Napier boys their asses*, Autumn thought.

"I'll stay in contact with you," she assured David.

He walked toward the door, then stopped and turned back.

"Listen, I want you girls to stay away from the woods for the next few weeks. There's somethin' been tearin' up deer out by the quarry, somethin' big. Might could be a black bear, and if it is, I don't like how close it's gettin' to town. Deputies are on it, I've got 'em patrolling the edges, but best you be careful all the same."

"I never go out there," Tana said. "Too much wildlife for me."

Autumn thought about her date with Killian and wondered with a shudder how close they might have come to a monster in the trees, never knowing it was there. She'd have to warn him not to go on any more lone walks early in the morning.

On the heels of that, her mind suddenly pitched back to her dream, and she felt dizzy from the force of it: the image of Killian, naked and screaming at the moon.

Howling like a mad beast as blood streamed down his neck and chest.

***

Autumn tried to keep the unfamiliar feeling of excitement at bay every time she thought of Killian. Between his odd behavior at the end of their date and her terrifying dream, she knew holding onto some youthful crush was silly and ill-advised. *Besides*, she reminded herself on Friday afternoon, *he hasn't called, hasn't stopped by. He probably decided to go back to Seattle.*

The thought pained her more than she liked to admit to herself. What was it about him? Why had she been pulled so easily into his orbit? It was almost shameful, how worked up she'd allowed herself to become over a man she likely wouldn't see again.

Tana noticed her silence and wisely decided to let it go, opting instead for a deli cookie left on the corner of Autumn's desk. A small reason to smile.

That evening, Autumn laid out the clothes she wanted to wear to Tommy's funeral and took a long, hot bath to try and ease some of the knots from her shoulders. In whorls of steam, she laid back and attempted to clear her mind, to rid herself of Killian.

Instead, she pulled him right into her dream.

It was unlike her previous vision. This was bizarre and uncomfortable in ways that didn't make sense. There was blood again, but it trickled and swelled from the ground like a hidden spring. By the light of the moon, it was an ever-changing burgundy that made Autumn thirsty for wine. When Killian appeared, he paid her no notice. Instead, he began digging into the soil with his bare hands, throwing dirt over the stream of blood as though he wanted to dry it up.

Then the dream changed, and she was floating over her seven-year-old self sitting in her bedroom surrounded by her stuffed animal collection. It was something she often did after her mother died: create a fortress of dolls and bears and sock monkeys, an impenetrable wall of friends who could protect her. They sat on her bed as she colored a picture, and adult-Autumn recalled the feeling of safety she'd had. Nothing could touch her when those stuffed animals were around, especially at night.

Daddy told me to stay put, she remembered suddenly, and a great wave of unease rolled over her. This was the day the bad thing happened.

From her spot near the ceiling, adult-Autumn heard a heavy *thump* from outside. She watched as her younger self looked up from her picture, head turned curiously. She saw her jump at the sudden loud bang that issued from the front yard.

I thought it was a firecracker, she remembered. *I wanted to see it.*

Her small child's body crawled over the stuffed animals and jumped down from the bed. Adult Autumn tried to shout at her to stop, but nothing happened. Child Autumn walked to her bedroom window and pulled aside the curtain, peering out into the darkness with an expectant smile on her face. There were no fireworks. There was only her father and another man standing over a dark lump that lay in their dusty front yard. The body of a man.

Her father jerked his head up and looked directly at her, cold eyes piercing her even in the moonless night.

Autumn woke slowly, groggy and disoriented from the heat of the bathwater. For a dizzying moment, she was sure someone was in the house with her, that her father had found her and broken in. She almost expected to see his short white beard glistening in the darkness of her bedroom beyond the bathroom door.

"Hello?" she called softly. Her heart pounded so hard it made her voice shiver.

Silence. In the distance, a dog barked once, twice.

She dried off quickly and pulled on a pair of black underwear and an old t-shirt, then grabbed the knife she kept in her coat pocket. Then she walked purposefully through the house to make sure all the doors and windows were locked. She liked to think of herself as someone who wasn't easily rattled, but the past week had done a number on her mental state. The ancient, crumbling two-story house she called home suddenly seemed less comforting than it ever had before.

Autumn had no idea why she'd settled on it when she was looking for a place to buy the previous year. It needed a lot of work, only some of which had been completed. The backyard was still a tangled and overgrown mess, the roof leaked, and the attic still held items from previous tenants. There was something about it though, a sort of vintage charm that lent itself well to her sense of style. There was a lovely stained-glass window over the kitchen sink depicting an orchid with verdant leaves, and a dumbwaiter connecting the kitchen and master bedroom that still worked. The first project she'd tackled upon moving in was the den, which was transformed into a library complete with floor-to-ceiling shelves in dark mahogany and a mercury glass chandelier Tana had rescued from a thrift store. Autumn had splurged on a comfy leather chair for the room and often fell asleep there when she was reading.

The rest of the house was cozy. Colorful throw rugs, soft, squashy furniture, and tons of framed pieces done by her friends and local artists. If she had more money and time, she would undoubtedly turn the house into something straight out of a Victorian murder mystery, but until then, she liked what she'd created. It was unique, and best of all, it was *hers*. It was something her father had never laid eyes upon.

When she was satisfied the house was secure, Autumn went upstairs and opened her bedroom window, just enough to let some cool air slip in. The evening was quiet except for an occasional dog barking across the neighborhood. She wrapped herself up in the purple quilt on her bed and lay back, wishing she had more control over her mind. It seemed that no matter what she did, Killian managed to jump back in there.

Not only that, her father was a recurring figure in her brain even after years of efforts to keep him out.

She closed her eyes and focused on Killian's face as she pushed herself toward sleep. If she had to concentrate on him to block her father, she'd gladly do so.

***

Autumn drove to the cemetery under cloudy skies, trying to fend off her nerves with a thermos of hot tea.

"Do you want me to go with you? We can shut down the office for an hour," Tana had said as Autumn was preparing to leave.

"Nah, I'll be fine," Autumn said. "But I appreciate your offer."

They hugged fiercely, and Tana pulled back to look at her friend with a smile.

"Do good but take no shit," she said. Their unofficial motto.

A cold wind had whipped up by the time Autumn got to her car, and she turned the heat up so that it whispered against her stockinged legs knowing it would be worse at the hillside gravesite.

Tommy had a modest turnout at the cemetery. Autumn figured most of the people who showed up for the church service had gone home afterward which left her feeling particularly exposed as she walked up the hill. She spotted Brooke right away; her pale, bobbed head shone like a beacon across the dim afternoon. Rose sat beside her in a folding chair. They held hands, clinging to one another like two doomed and drowning loved ones.

"Autumn," Brooke cried, running over for a hug.

"Hey, you," Autumn said. She knelt to Brooke's eye level, unmindful of the damp ground beneath her knee. "How are you feeling today?"

"I'm okay," Brooke said. "Uncle Bill brought his dogs over this morning so we could play. They ate a bunch of crabapples and pooped everywhere. It was still fun, though."

"Oh my goodness," Autumn said. "That sounds like a big mess, but I'm glad you got to play for a little while."

"Thank you for comin'," Rose said when Autumn walked Brooke back to her seat. "I wasn't sure you would."

"I'm happy to do it," said Autumn. "How are you feeling today?"

Rose inclined her head and looked away, over the gravesite and past the trees beyond. She didn't like being reminded of her condition. The dark circles beneath her eyes were so pronounced they looked painted on. Autumn wondered if she'd slept at all.

"I'm alright. A little tired is all."

"Can I do anything for you? Something to make you more comfortable?" Autumn asked.

"Not unless you've got a new body to donate," Rose said, then seemed to realize how dark her humor was. "Thank you, but I'm okay. This shouldn't take too long."

There were a few familiar faces in the small crowd that had gathered. Autumn recognized Brooke's teacher, Garth Thompson, as well as Amelia Hobarts, who owned the flower shop Rose worked at before she became too ill. She scanned the figures standing along the treeline at the back of the cemetery and thought she recognized Bill and Austin Napier, their dark heads bent toward one another conspiratorially. They were both muscular and in dark suits, so she couldn't tell which was which, but she suddenly felt with absolute certainty that they were talking about her. She felt a stab of panic before realizing they were just sharing nips from a small silver flask.

"Idiots," Rose hissed, and Autumn realized she understood what they were doing, too.

When Reverend Shelby began the service, Autumn turned to walk to the back of the congregation, but Brooke grabbed her hand and held her where she was. For a long moment, she debated pulling away as gently as possible and making a quick exit, but she couldn't leave the little girl. Not when her father was moments away from being cast into the earth.

She sat down gingerly in the last chair in the front row, still holding Brooke's hand. There were prayers, sniffles, comforting words in the reverend's low monotone. Rose remained stoic but Brooke swiped at her eyes a few times. She seemed to be trying to stay strong for her mother, and Autumn felt a sharp tug in her gut at that.

They watched as the coffin was slowly lowered into its hole. Overhead, a murder of crows swept by shouting cries of indignation, as though they objected to the funeral. Brooke leaned against Autumn's arm and hummed quietly under her breath, a version of "You Are My Sunshine". Autumn kept her eyes cast downward as people made their way over to give Rose their final condolences, trying not to attract attention. After a few moments, she looked at Brooke and gently squeezed her hand.

"You okay, Little Bee?" Autumn whispered. "You know it's okay to cry if you feel like it, right?"

Brooke nodded. "I'm okay. A little tired." It was almost exactly what Rose had said. Brooke was taking cues from her mother on how to react to the situation.

"Did you drive here today?" Autumn asked Rose. "If not, I can give you guys a ride home, stop and get some food if you want."

"She don't need your help," Bill Napier said loudly, walking up to the row of chairs to stand in front of Autumn. "She's got family for that."

Autumn looked up to meet his eyes. Austin stood behind him, glaring at her. Her stomach tensed and she pushed her panic away, knowing if she showed fear they'd smell it like dogs.

"I didn't mean to overstep," she said evenly. "I only came because Brooke asked me to."

A muscle in Austin's jaw flexed and he shook his head, turning away as though he wanted to say something. He seemed to be waiting for a cue from his brother, but Bill remained still, hands at his sides. There was a small white scar above his left eye, probably the result of some barfight. He had the sort of hard good looks all the Napier men boasted. In another life, Autumn would have found him attractive. In this one, she found him only to be a repulsive bully.

"You think sitting here in the front row ain't overstepping?" Bill asked roughly. "Like you're one of the family? Who the hell told you that was okay?"

"That's enough," came a voice on Autumn's left. She turned to see David walking toward them, hands resting on his gun belt, forehead furrowed. "Miss Phillips is here in an official capacity, and you'd do well to remember that as an employee of the state, she's more than welcome here or anywhere else in town she decides to visit."

"It's very simple. This is a private family event," Austin said loudly, pointing his finger at Autumn. "She's not welcome here. We have rights, goddammit."

"I'm leaving," Autumn said, standing up. She bent in front of Brooke and held the girl's hands in hers, looking her in the eyes. "It's okay, Bee. You go home and get some rest and I'll see you on Monday, okay?"

She'd been afraid that Brooke would cry and protest, that she would cling tightly and refuse to let her leave, but Brooke only nodded. Her thumb hovered near her mouth, then fell into her lap.

Autumn took Rose's cool, dry hands briefly into her own and murmured her condolences, then walked away from the gravesite with David.

"I'm sorry I couldn't get here quicker," he said. "Deputies have kept me busy all morning."

"Did you find the bear?"

David shook his head. "No bear. But there were signs in the woods of somethin' big. We might have some more killing before the weekend is over."

For some reason, his words sent a shiver through Autumn. She wrapped her arms around herself and contemplated the bruised sky feeling a weight of sorrow for Brooke. She hated leaving the girl here amid all this grief.

"I gotta head back out. You gonna be okay?" David asked.

"Sure. Thanks for bailing me out back there."

He smiled and touched her elbow. "No worries. Those boys are more bark than bite, but their bark ain't so nice, for sure."

She watched him walk down the hill to his patrol car, then turned and headed for her car. She'd parked on the side of one of the cemetery's many access roads, which backed up to a grove of trees, and she was imagining how nice it would be to get back into the warm office with Tana when a strong hand closed over her wrist.

Autumn whirled around, her hand automatically going for the knife in her coat.

"Nope, you don't," Bill said. The smile on his face was more terrifying than any of the glaring looks he'd given her in the past. He jammed his hand into her pocket and pulled out the knife, then slung it into the underbrush.

"Not so brave when you don't have the police chief here to fight your battles for you," said Austin. He circled both of them, eyes shifting warily to either side of the tree line to watch for witnesses.

"This isn't necessary," Autumn said, fighting to keep the tremor out of her voice. "I'm going to be out of Brooke's life soon, but the state will only transfer her into the care of another social worker. It's best for everyone if you just cooperate..."

"Nah, we don't have to cooperate," Bill said, tightening his grip on her wrist. "Don't you know who we are?"

She heard Austin laugh, saw Bill raise his fist to the sky. His arm was bent at the elbow, ready to deliver a blow. Autumn closed her eyes and turned her head, waiting for the world to explode in blinding pain, and felt Bill's hand detach roughly from hers. She opened her eyes again in time to see him go flying across the road and into a tombstone.

"Hey," Austin cried, confused.

Autumn blinked and turned around with hands raised to guard her face. It was unnecessary. Killian stood between her and Bill, fists clenched at his sides. chest heaving, a look of murderous rage etched across his face.

Chapter Five

"Leave," Killian said to Austin. His voice was pitched low, barely controlled, and his hands were curled into hard fists at his sides.

"Hey, fuck you, buddy," Austin said, advancing on him. "Who the hell do you think you are?"

"I'm the guy who steps in when he sees two assholes assaulting a woman," Killian said through clenched teeth. "Don't make me be the guy who has to nurse a broken hand later."

Austin slowed as he got closer to Killian, seemed to realize he was outmuscled, and gave him a wide berth as he walked toward his brother. Bill was getting up, holding a hand over his nose.

"You broke it," he said in a muffled voice. "You broke my nose, you asshole."

"Good," said Killian. "Every time you look in the mirror, I want you to remember this day and all the choices you made and how they were bad ones. You feel me?"

Bill glared at him. Hatred shimmered in the air between them like heat over blacktop. Afraid things would escalate, she scanned below the hill for David, but he was long gone.

"This ain't over," Bill mumbled as he walked away. Austin followed, throwing one last murderous glance over his shoulder at both of them.

Autumn turned to Killian with wide eyes.

"Where did you come from?"

"I was on a walk and saw you drive up to the cemetery. Thought I'd meet you at your car to see if you were okay. Who the hell were those yahoos?"

"The richest men in town," Autumn said, retrieving her knife from the bushes. "They're also the uncles of one of my clients. Her father was buried today."

"Why were they attacking you?"

"They don't like me butting in," she said tiredly. "I guess they were trying to scare me off."

He closed the distance between them and took her arm gently in his hand, bringing her hand palm-up to inspect her wrist.

"Are you okay?"

There was no pushing away the heat that swirled up at his touch. Autumn watched his face; he was gazing intently at her wrist, not paying attention to her expression, and she had time to see how beautiful his features were.

"I'm fine," she said after a moment. "I would have been fine. I know how to handle myself against assholes. But thank you for stepping in."

He let go of her and nodded. "I know you do. But you have no idea how hard it was for me to let that guy walk away after he put his hands on you like that."

She looked up, into his eyes, and saw that the rage was still there, diluted only slightly.

"Where have you been? I thought you went back to Seattle," she said.

"Something came up," he said. "I didn't mean to disappear. It's complicated."

"Oh," she said. "Does that mean you're staying in Pine Hollow?"

"I don't know yet. But I'd like to spend some time with you again if you're open to it."

Something inside her chest opened up, like a flower in the rain.

"Yes," she said with a smile. "Are you free tonight? You could come over for dinner."

"I'd love that. Can I bring anything?"

"Yourself. What do you like to eat?"

"Anything at all, I'm not picky."

They began walking toward her car. A line of vehicles wound down the hill as mourners left the service and she knew Brooke was in one of them, leaving behind her father for good. The thought sobered her and Killian seemed to sense her change in mood, lightly touching her back as they reached the car.

"You sure you're okay?" he asked.

"Yeah, I'm alright. A little worried for my client. She's had a hard life, and it keeps getting harder."

"I'm sorry to hear that. She's lucky to have you, then."

She smiled up at him, grateful for the kindness. "I'm the lucky one. I'm glad to have her in my life, even if it does bring the occasional unpleasantness."

"There's that good heart rearing up," Killian said and touched her cheek lightly with one finger. "See you at seven?"

"Perfect," Autumn said softly.

She watched him walk down the hill, hands tucked tightly into his pockets, and knew the rest of the day was going to drag by.

***

"Well, you were right about the Napiers," Autumn said as she walked into the office.

"Shit." Tana winced. "What happened?"

"Austin and Bill got upset that I sat beside Brooke at the service, started talking shit, so David got them to back off," said Autumn as she collapsed into her chair. "Then they followed me to my car and tried to jump me."

"Are you fucking kidding?" Tana cried, jumping up. "I'm calling David right now..."

"No, no, it's okay. They didn't have time to do much before Killian showed up."

Tana faltered. "What? He showed up to the funeral?"

"Not to the service. He said he was on a walk and saw me drive up, and he was going to wait by my car to make sure everything was okay. He didn't know about Tommy."

Tana sat down again. Autumn could almost see visions of Killian's massive frame dancing in her eyes. "So what happened?"

"He threw Bill into a headstone. I'm pretty sure he broke his nose."

"What?" Tana cried. "Oh, Jesus, Autumn, this is not good. The Napiers have a long memory, and they hold grudges."

"I know," Autumn said. "But they kind of slunk away with their tails between their legs. Neither of them wanted to mess with Killian. It was kind of scary and completely awesome."

"You said they jumped you. What exactly did they do?"

"Well, Bill grabbed me. Had his fist up like he was ready to punch me. Lucky for me, Killian got there when he did."

Tana got up and walked over to Autumn, wrapping her arms around her friend's shoulders in a tight hug. She stayed there for a long moment, then perched on the edge of Autumn's desk.

"Are you okay?"

"I'm fine. I even got another date for tonight. He's coming over for dinner, although I'm not sure what I'm going to make yet. It all happened so fast."

She was talking rapidly, stumbling over her words, but it couldn't be helped. It was a symptom of her anxiety because now that she was back in the safety of her office, the day's events seemed to hit her all at once. As soon as Tana asked if she was alright, tears welled up in her throat and stuck there.

Tana was shaking her head. "I shouldn't have let you go alone."

"Don't," Autumn said firmly and swallowed hard. "Don't do that to yourself. I'm fine, and Bill and Austin can hold a grudge all they want. They're not going to scare me off. I owe it to Brooke to keep doing my job."

"This scares me, Autumn. The fact that they were willing to attack you in a place where anyone might have seen...what will they do next?"

"I can't think about that," Autumn said, but she'd already thought about it. The worry nagged at her until the workday was over.

***

After work, Autumn hurried beneath cloudy skies to pick up the things she needed from the grocery. Luckily, the house was already pretty clean. A lit candle and some open windows created a fragrance inside the rooms that was one part fall leaves and one part cinnamon roll. She turned some music on low in the kitchen and started the pasta so it could boil while she was showering, keeping her fingers crossed that Killian liked Italian food.

By the time she was clean and ready, in a simple black wrap dress with her long hair winding down her back, the pasta was done. She added sausage, tomatoes, onions, olive oil, and herbs to a skillet over low heat and made sure the bottle of wine she'd bought was chilled.

At five minutes to seven, the doorbell rang. She padded barefoot to the front door and stood motionless for a moment, trying to calm the nerves that felt like frayed wires in her belly.

"Hi," she said softly when she pulled the door open.

"Hello," Killian said with a smile. He shook his head as he looked her up and down. "You look...I was trying to find a word better than beautiful, but that's all I can come up with."

Autumn laughed. "Well, thank you. So do you. Look beautiful, I mean. Not beautiful, I didn't mean that. You look very handsome."

Her nervousness was yanking at her tongue again. She forced herself to take a deep breath and stood aside so he could come in. He looked better than she dared to say, in a black t-shirt that showed off his muscular arms and black jeans.

"These are for you," he said, handing her a bouquet of exquisite white orchids.

"Oh," Autumn breathed. "These are—I don't know what to say. They're gorgeous. Where did you find orchids around here?"

He shrugged. "Lady at the florist special ordered them for a wedding. I sweet-talked her into selling me some. I thought these suit you better than roses."

"They absolutely do," she said and brought them to her face to breathe in deeply. They smelled like secrets in the dark. "Thank you so much."

"It smells amazing in here," he said, looking around for the source. "I hope you made a lot of whatever it is you're cooking."

Autumn laughed and led him through the living room and into the kitchen, where she stood on tiptoe to reach a vase from an upper cabinet.

"I always make too much ziti, so there's plenty," she said, struggling to grasp the glass vase.

"Here, let me help with that," Killian said.

His fingers closed over hers for a millisecond before picking up the vase and handing it gently to her. Their bodies were only inches apart; the heat of his chest radiated against her arm and she recalled how warm he'd been on the night she showed him around town. It was the kind of warmth that made her think of flushed skin and whispers in the darkness, and she shivered uncontrollably.

"Are you cold? I can close some windows for you," he said. His voice was even deeper than usual, pitched low because they were so close.

"No, I'm fine," she said. She took the vase from him and cleared her throat. "Would you like some wine?"

"Love some," he said, looking around. "I like your house."

"Thanks," Autumn said, feeling a blush creep into her cheeks. She didn't have many visitors, and now that Killian was here—an architect seeing her private things, walking through the rooms she lived in—it all suddenly felt *small*. "As you can see, I focus mainly on comfort when I'm home."

"That's the best kind of home," he said kindly, smiling at her. "It's—and I don't use this word often—*lovely*. Lots of air and light. It suits you. Was this your family's house?"

Autumn felt the smile fall from her face and struggled to keep her tone light.

"No, I don't have much family anymore. My father's still in town, but we don't speak."

"I'm sorry; I didn't mean to..."

"No, no, it's okay," she assured him. "My mom died when I was seven. She was an only child, and her parents died before I was born. My father's family, what little there is, all moved to Oregon years ago."

"Can I ask how long you've been on your own?" His voice was gentle.

"Since I was sixteen," she said. "I graduated high school early, got emancipated, moved into a little apartment with Tana. She had a great home life, but her parents were all about letting her make her own decisions, so they were supportive."

"Wow. Sixteen. I can't imagine being on my own when I was that age. It takes a special kind of person to do that."

Autumn shrugged off his compliment as she handed him a glass of wine. "My father was too wrapped up in his business to care what I did. It was a pretty toxic environment. I'm grateful to him for not giving a shit because otherwise I'd have been stuck there."

He watched her for a moment, studying her face. It might have been uncomfortable with anyone else, but with him, it was only intense. Autumn gazed into his eyes and wondered, for the hundredth time, what this man saw in her.

"That's enough about me," she said with a little laugh. "What about you? Tell me everything."

His face changed then, from gentle and happy to melancholy, although he never lost his smile. The change happened in his eyes, and Autumn was sorry she'd asked.

"My family is pretty great," he said simply. "Mom and Dad were high school sweethearts and they were pretty laid-back parents when I was growing up. We lived in a small town, so I rode my bike everywhere. I had a few cousins who lived close, so I always had someone to hang out with."

"I'm jealous," Autumn joked. She bent and checked on the ziti, which was bubbling in the oven. "That sounds wonderful. Are your parents…"

"Mom passed two years ago, Dad about six months ago."

"Oh, god. I'm so sorry."

"It's okay. They both went peacefully, with no illness or pain. That's all you can ask for, right?"

"Amen to that," Autumn said softly. She suddenly realized this must be the reason for his sadness; he was looking to move to get away from his grief. For one brief, agonizing second, she felt the strongest urge to hug him as tightly as she could.

Instead, she boldly took his hand in hers for the barest moment and squeezed it before turning to take dinner out of the oven. When she turned around, she found him staring openly at her, his brow furrowed into a frown.

"What's wrong?" she asked, setting the pan on the stove so she could move closer to him.

"Bruises," he said, and his voice sounded strangled. "On your arm."

She looked down, confused, and saw dark finger-marks on her forearm. Bill's finger-marks. She looked back up at Killian and spoke softly.

"It's okay. I didn't even know they were there."

"It's not okay," he said. His expression was stormy. "If I see him again I'll break his goddamn arm."

"No, please," Autumn said, alarmed. She put both hands on his chest, lightly, and looked into his eyes. "Bill Napier is a bully, but his father is a very powerful man around here. He could make trouble for me in a hundred ways, most of them professionally. Please don't be upset about this. I swear, I'm fine."

He looked down at her for a long moment, then breathed heavily through his nose. "Alright. But if he comes around or threatens you again, I want you to tell me. Promise me."

She wouldn't do any such thing, but she nodded anyway. "Okay."

***

"I can honestly say that was one of the best meals of my life," Killian said, leaning back in his chair. "Where the hell did you learn to cook like that?"

"Tana's mom taught me," Autumn said, delighted he'd enjoyed it. "She came over every weekend when we lived together and taught us a new recipe. Said if we were going to live on our own, we had to learn how to take care of ourselves and eat right. She's an amazing person."

"Sounds like it. Seriously, this meal was incredible. Thank you so much," he said. "I've had a lot of fast food lately so this was a rare treat."

"Oh, well, anytime you feel like having a home-cooked meal, you're more than welcome here."

It was a bold invitation for her, but he seemed genuinely grateful for it.

"I thought maybe we could sit outside on the front porch for a bit," she said. "It's a lovely night."

Killian laughed. "It's cold and cloudy."

"Exactly. My favorite kind of night," she said with a smile.

Autumn grabbed a lighter, the bottle of wine, and their glasses as she led him outside. Clouds were gathering overhead, amassing an army. The leaves left on the trees rattled in the wind as she lit a few candles and refilled their glasses.

The only chair on the porch was a deep wicker two-seater that boasted a comfy cushion. Killian sat gingerly, clearly afraid to put all his weight on it, and Autumn chuckled.

"I know it's wicker, but it's super sturdy, I promise," she said, handing him his glass. "I reinforced the bottom after I bought it at a yard sale."

"I don't know, I'm pretty heavy," he said. "Think it can hold both of us?"

"Absolutely," she said and wrapped her arms around herself. The thin cotton dress she'd chosen wasn't ideal for fall weather. "You know, on second thought, maybe I should grab a sweater."

She turned to go back inside but he grabbed her hand and pulled her gently down into his lap, wrapping his thick arms around her waist. She gasped and braced herself against his chest. Their faces were so close she could see tiny flecks of gold in his dark eyes. The candle flames, she realized.

"I can keep you warm," he said. His voice was a deep rumble in his chest. "Unless you'd just prefer a sweater."

"No," she cried quickly, and he laughed and pulled her tighter into him, bringing a hand up to cradle her cheek. When his mouth found hers, she moaned softly and placed both hands on his face, running her fingers through his beard before bringing them around to stroke the back of his neck.

He was so *warm*. Like a furnace, she mused, closing her eyes as his tongue danced along with hers. They quickly found a rhythm. Killian moved his hands softly up and down her back and she shivered in response, feeling gooseflesh break out on her arms. When he pulled away and began lightly kissing the line of her jaw, she tilted her head back, and he made his way down her throat all the way to her clavicle. Her reaction was intense and immediate; a deep, aching throb settled in between her legs, more powerful than she'd ever felt before. She clung tightly to him as the world spun around her.

It was her turn. She sat up and gently kissed the corner of his mouth. Moved to his cheek, the curve of his jaw, his ear. He took a sharp breath when she licked his earlobe and held her tighter; she could feel how hard he was and figured that was one of his favorite spots. When she began lightly scratching the back of his neck, he moaned and closed his eyes. More kisses, this time on his throat. She ran a hand across his chest, rubbed a thumb across his nipple, then dived down and lifted his shirt for some skin-on-skin contact. As soon as her hand touched his hard stomach, he sucked in a breath and brought her back to his mouth, holding the back of her head with one strong hand.

"Christ," he growled when they finally broke apart. "If we don't stop, I'm going to embarrass myself."

"Me too," Autumn said as she tried to catch her breath. "I'm sorry if I went too far—"

He quieted her with a look. "I'm the one who pulled you into my lap. Which I apologize for, by the way. I don't know what came over me. I hope I didn't scare you."

"Not at all," she said with a smile. "I've been waiting for this since the night we walked around town."

"I'm glad I'm not the only one."

Her stomach fluttered at that, and she leaned against him burying her face into his neck so he wouldn't see how flushed her cheeks were. In the warm circle of his arms, with the pending storm whipping the air around them, she felt impossibly good. Impossibly safe.

"I hope this doesn't ruin the mood, but..." she began, and faltered, unsure of how to phrase her question. "I was wondering if you've made a decision yet. About moving here."

He tensed up and she immediately regretted asking. How stupid could she be? They'd only known each other for a week and she was already trying to get him to live there. He probably thought she was clingy, pushy, overbearing...

"I'm pretty sure I'm going to move here," he said, cutting off her thoughts. Relief flooded through her so quickly she felt light-headed. "But I want to be honest with you about something."

She sat up and looked at him, already thinking the worst: he would tell her he was married, or that he was only looking for a good time. A thousand other possibilities flew through her head until she felt dizzy.

"I had other reasons for coming to Pine Hollow," he said finally. "I'm looking for someone."

She digested that for a moment. "Well if you need some help, I know most of the people who live here."

He shook his head. "It's not something I want to get you involved in. It's a volatile situation, and I won't put you in danger."

"Danger?" she said, her brows knitting in concern. "Killian, please don't put yourself in harm's way. I know the chief of police, we can help..."

"No," he said firmly. "I appreciate the offer, but there's no way in hell I'm going to stick you in the middle of it. Besides, I don't have a name or much information about the person, anyway. And what I do know...I can't tell you."

"Oh," she said softly. "I don't know if I even have a right to say this, but please be careful. Pine Hollow is a nice town, but there's a darkness here just like anywhere else. If something happened to you…"

He brought her close again and kissed her gently on the lips, stroking her cheek with his thumb. "I'll be fine. I promise."

She nodded and wrapped her arms around his neck, wishing she was bold enough to ask him to stay.

As if on cue, Killian looked at his watch. "It's late. I should get going."

Autumn glanced at her phone and was astonished to see that they'd been sitting on the porch for two hours. The night was completely dark around them, the wind whispering through the trees ahead of the storm that still hadn't broken the atmosphere.

She stood up on shaky legs and crossed her arms over her breasts, suddenly freezing now that she was out of his reach.

"Thank you so much for dinner," he said, brushing her hair away from her face. "You have no idea how much it meant to me."

"I meant what I said about you coming over any time," she said softly.

"I will definitely take you up on that."

"Tomorrow?" Her voice lilted hopefully.

"I might not be able to come around for a couple of days."

She felt her face fall and was rewarded with a gentle kiss.

"No sadness, please, I can't take that look on your face. It breaks my heart," he said with a little smile. "I'm going to have to travel a little, to a few towns close by. But I'll be back on Sunday night. Might be late, though."

"Then I'll make something that tastes good reheated," she said, and when he bent to hug her, he lifted her off her feet and held her to him.

"I don't know how I found you," he whispered against her ear. "But goddamn, I'm so glad I did."

Chapter Six

Autumn woke the next morning with the strangest, strongest feeling that the previous night had been one long, incredible dream. She brought her fingers to her lips and traced them, remembering the feel of Killian's mouth and how tightly he'd pressed her to him. The familiar,

sweet ache began again and she groaned. She had no idea how she was going to get through a

long weekend without seeing him.

After a hot shower, she threw on some comfy sweats and padded downstairs. The storm threatening them the night before had broken while she was asleep, leaving behind rain-tinted air and overcast skies. She raised a couple of windows and put the tea kettle on when her phone rang.

"I'm getting out of town and I'm taking you with me," Tana said when she answered.

"What?" Autumn laughed. "Where are you going?"

"*We* are going to Cedarville. My mom invited us down to the lake house for the weekend. We're going to make s'mores, we're going to decorate the place for fall, and we're going to forget about our worries the entire time."

"I don't know," Autumn said. "I should probably try to get some work done around the house—"

"I know you are not standing in your living room in those ratty-ass sweats telling me that you're turning down an invitation to *the lake house.*"

Autumn frowned and spun in a circle, looking out the windows. "Can you see me right now?"

"No, but I know you better than anyone," Tana said, laughing. "Come on. It'll make me happy. We can stop on the way and pick up some wine and chocolate."

Autumn smiled and considered the previous night when the wine had led to some lovely things. She didn't want to be stuck in a lake house without Killian all weekend with those memories keeping her worked up.

"Make it whiskey and we'll talk," she said.

***

"I can't believe you guys didn't do it," Tana said disbelievingly from behind the wheel.

She'd offered to drive since her SUV was more reliable than Autumn's car, and now she peered over the steering wheel to try and focus on the road through a sheet of rain. She'd demanded every detail of Autumn's date with Killian, no matter how distracting.

"I wanted to, believe me," said Autumn. "He did, too. It just wasn't the right time. We're still getting to know each other."

"When does he get back from this mysterious trip?"

"Tomorrow night. He said he'd come over."

"Did you feel like he was being straight with you?"

"Yes. He brought it up, said he wanted to be honest about why he was here. But he's still keeping a lot to himself. I didn't want to pry, but it's killing me to be so in the dark about what he's doing, especially since he said it's dangerous."

"Yeah, I don't like that part at all. You need to be careful around him, Autumn. I liked him when we met, and I know how you feel about him, but that doesn't mean he won't turn out to be trouble."

"I know." Autumn sighed. "I almost wish I didn't like him so much. It would make things easier."

Tana seemed to be on the verge of saying something, but the turnoff for the lake house came up suddenly, forcing her to slow down. She maneuvered the SUV down a small gravel lane rutted with weeds and after a moment, the sprawling white house came into view.

It was a stunning piece of property, sitting right on the lake. The house included a wraparound porch that boasted half a dozen rocking chairs and heavy iron lanterns, lit for their arrival. The rain slowed to a sprinkle as Tana parked at the far end of the house and turned to Autumn.

"We're home," she said with a smile.

Tana's mother, Sylvia, was waiting at the door, arms folded for warmth against the chill of the day. She smiled as they walked up, burdened with their bags, and pushed open the door for them.

"My girls," she said warmly. "Did you have to drive in that awful storm that just passed through?"

"A little bit," Tana said, dumping her stuff by the door to free her arms for a hug. "Where's Dad?"

"In the kitchen, finishing up dinner. We've got steak, chicken, twice-baked potatoes, grilled Brussels sprouts with garlic and honey, wild green salad, and that rye bread you like."

Autumn's stomach rumbled at the mere mention of all that food; the house smelled incredible. She waited impatiently for her turn at a hug and was rewarded with a gentle embrace redolent of Sylvia's comforting scent of blackberries and lavender.

"How are you, my girl?" Sylvia asked softly. She pulled back to look at Autumn, her dark eyes searching for any signs of unhappiness. She'd changed her hair since Autumn had seen her last—shoulder-length waves rather than the box braids she usually favored—but other than that she looked virtually unchanged, a glowing beauty who never wore makeup because she didn't need it.

"I'm good," Autumn said with a smile. She didn't want to bring her job here, no matter how sympathetic an ear Sylvia had.

"Hmm," said Sylvia, peering intently into Autumn's eyes. "No, not entirely, but you don't have to talk about it now. We have all night."

She'd always had an eerie insight into their moods. It did no good to cover up emotions with Sylvia because she always sussed it out.

She led Autumn into the kitchen, where Tana was embracing her father. He was tall so she tilted her chin up to look at him, face illuminated by the warm glow of the overhead lights, and Autumn felt a sudden pang of jealousy twinge her abdomen. *To be held and loved by your father*, she thought viciously. *What a concept.*

"Autumn," Greg called, extending an arm to invite her in for a hug. "Get over here, girl."

"Hey, Greg," she said, smiling, suddenly ashamed of her envy.

"You hungry? You better be, because Sylvia made me cook enough to feed an army," Greg said as he gave her his patented quick squeeze.

"Starving," she said.

Things were informal with the Jones. A stack of clean white plates sat at the end of the counter beside paper napkins and a basket of silverware, while the dishes of food were arranged buffet-style so that everyone could serve themselves. It took a practiced eye to notice the plates were vintage Wedgwood and the flatware was real silver, passed down through generations.

Greg, a surgeon, and Sylvia, a psychiatrist and professor, had worked hard to give their only daughter every comfort and opportunity and had managed to keep her from becoming a spoiled brat because they were incredibly loving, generous, and open-minded. Autumn had counted them as foster parents since she was a teenager and was grateful to have them in her life.

Once plates were filled, they moved to the dinner table situated at the far end of the kitchen beside a floor-to-ceiling bay window. The lake churned beneath the rain as mist hovered in the distance, blurring the trees. The conversation was light, no job talk at all, but rather stories from the family's summer vacation to Texas and about Sylvia's newest project, teaching cooking classes at the local senior center.

"So many seniors don't know how to cook healthy meals for themselves, and they miss out on the vital nutrients they need because they end up going for what's easiest, which is fast food or prepackaged meals," Sylvia said. "If I can teach them how to shop and put together a nutritious meal that tastes good, it might help their quality of life and boost their self-esteem a little."

"That's so incredible," Autumn said. "They couldn't ask for a better teacher. I made your ziti for a friend last night and he said it was the best meal he'd ever eaten."

"Save your praise until you've eaten dessert," Tana warned, pointing her fork at the refrigerator. When her mother gave her a sly smile, Tana said, "Don't think I didn't notice that Death By Chocolate cake."

"I was going to surprise you," Sylvia said, laughing. "I wanted to make a special dessert because we're going to have company in a bit."

"Oh yeah? Not one of your shrink friends, I hope," Tana said, and made a gagging gesture at Autumn, who laughed.

"*No*, not one of my incredibly interesting and amazing "shrink friends"," Sylvia said. "She's a guest lecturer at the university this month. Claire Roberts. An expert in the field of divination, tarot, and palmistry."

"Ooh, this is gonna be good," Tana said, rubbing her hands together. "Will she read for us?"

"I'd say she could be persuaded," Sylvia said. "Although I'll have to kick your dad out. He thinks she's loony."

"I never said "loony"," Greg said, holding his hands up at chest level in defense. "I said she was a little odd, that's all. The woman brought sage into your office and made a big deal about "cleansing" it before she could sit down. You don't think that's weird?"

"Sometimes a little weird is entirely welcome," Sylvia said airily, inclining her head. Autumn saw Tana in the gesture and smiled broadly, loving the interaction, the warm and playful back-and-forth.

"Well I'm excited to meet her," she said. "I've never had my palm read, it'll be fun."

"You can tell me all about it after she's gone," Greg said with a laugh. "I'll be in the bedroom watching Netflix in the meantime."

***

Claire Roberts looked nothing like Autumn imagined she would. She'd pictured a petite older woman draped in purple shawls, fingers weighed down by silver, maybe an artsy statement necklace. Instead, the woman who followed Sylvia into the kitchen soon after dinner looked to be a young and vibrant 40, clothed in chic dark jeans and a chambray button-down beneath a long cardigan. Her ash blonde hair fell to her shoulders.

"Hello," she said brightly when she entered. "You must be Tana and Autumn."

"It's so nice to meet you," Autumn said. "We're fascinated by what Sylvia's told us about your field of expertise."

"Does that mean you'll let me give you a reading?" Claire asked, looking from Autumn to Tana. "I already feel some really interesting energy in this room and I'm dying to explore it."

Tana shot a gleeful look at Autumn. "I don't think we'll let you leave until you do."

"Shall we go into the living room and get comfortable?" Sylvia asked.

"Only if you bring that cake," Tana said.

Autumn led the way and they settled on the plush white couches in the living room as the storm started cranking up again. Tana lit several candles and turned off the overhead lights as rain lashed at the windows. By the time Sylvia reappeared laden with a tray filled with cake plates, wine, and a carafe of coffee, the three of them were deep into a conversation about Claire's line of work.

"How did you get started? I mean, what drew you to it?" Tana asked.

"When I was a little girl, my grandmother told me all the time that I was special. I used to think it was because I was her only granddaughter, but as I got older I realized that she and I shared some gifts," Claire said. "She taught me tarot, how to read palms, how to listen to my instincts. That's ninety percent of what I do."

"And what's the other ten percent?" Autumn asked, leaning forward eagerly.

"Reading," Claire said with a laugh. "I've done so much research in the last ten years I could probably write five books."

"Claire is working on her Master's degree," Sylvia explained.

"There's a Master's for what you do?" Tana asked, awed.

"Well, technically it's in the area of religion with a focus on occult studies," Claire said. "If you're interested in learning how to read after this, I can teach you. It's not that difficult."

"Really?" Autumn asked.

"Most people think you have to be clairvoyant, but what you truly need to be is open. As it happens, I'm both, but there are many out there whose hearts and minds are open enough to excel at palmistry without the aid of other gifts."

Tana and Autumn exchanged a look, both excited at the prospect of learning to read palms.

"Who's going to go first?" Claire asked.

"Me," Autumn cried, at the same time Tana said, "I will,"

They laughed and Autumn sat back on the couch, content to watch despite her enthusiasm.

"You go," she said to Tana. "I'm going to eat my cake."

"Relax your hand, close your eyes, and try not to think about any *one* thing too hard," Claire said to Tana. "If I touch on something that rings true, don't give a sign. Wait until the end to ask questions, okay?"

Tana nodded and settled in eagerly, holding out her palm for Claire to take. They formed a lovely picture in the dim living room, illuminated by candlelight and framed by darkened windows. Sylvia watched with an open smile. Autumn wondered if she'd seen Claire at work before.

"You play an instrument," Claire said softly, gazing intently at Tana's upturned hand. "Guitar, I think. You recently spent time with someone who had a raised scar on their shoulder. I can feel it, the way you did."

Tana's mouth fell open in surprise, but she didn't open her eyes or speak.

"You're worried, in some secret way you can't name, that you'll be alone. But I see you married down the line. Married with two children. It won't be an easy road, but you'll get there,"

Claire said. "You are very fulfilled by your job. That's a rare find, especially in someone your age. You're going to continue to do great things for the people you serve."

When she sat back, Tana opened her eyes. She was crying.

"Thank you so much," she said, swiping at her eyes. "That was incredible."

"You're welcome. I told you, if you want to learn, I'm happy to teach you how to read. There are little clues that give you insight, such as the way someone holds their hand. For instance, when you opened your palm, your index and middle finger automatically curled inward. That told me that you play an instrument."

Tana looked at Autumn. "You have to try this."

Autumn set down her cake plate and switched places with Tana, suddenly feeling apprehensive. What would this woman see that no one else did? Was she skilled enough to ascertain Autumn's past? To see the trauma there?

"You ready?" Claire asked gently.

"Yes," said Autumn, and she took a deep breath.

Claire's hand was warm and soft. She cradled Autumn's palm and looked deeply at every crevice, every line, and fissure.

"I think the energy I felt in the kitchen earlier was coming from you," Claire murmured. "I've never met anyone like it."

"What do you mean?" Autumn asked, alarmed.

"Oh, nothing bad, not at all. There's something hidden in you, something that you or those closest to you might see as darkness."

There's a shadow in you, Autumn's grandma whispered in her mind.

"It's not, though," Claire said quickly. "It's more of an opening, the way a doorway can be darkened but not closed."

"I don't know what that means," Autumn said. Her voice shivered on the last word.

"It means you have abilities most people don't," Claire said, studying Autumn's palm intently. "Do you sleepwalk?"

"I don't think so."

"Do you have vivid dreams?"

"Yes, always. Since I was a kid."

Claire nodded. "I think you might be a traveler."

"A traveler?" Tana repeated. "Like, astral projection?"

"Yes. It's a rare gift, extremely rare, but I believe that's what I'm feeling here." She turned back to Autumn. "When you sleep, your subconscious self walks through that doorway and travels to other places, either locally or far away."

Autumn swallowed, hard, like a period at the end of a sentence. "I always called it Dream Country."

"Most people who travel don't realize they're doing it. They believe they have vivid dreams and that's where it ends. It can be quite dangerous because one could potentially get stuck or lost while projecting. Not only that, it's a process in which the soul leaves the body, meaning your physical form is left behind, unprotected. An empty vessel. If a demon or another being came along and needed a host, well, let's just say it wouldn't be ideal."

"And you think this is happening to Autumn?" Sylvia asked with a frown.

"I believe so, yes."

"What can I do? How do I protect myself?" Autumn asked.

"Well, the good news is that now you know Dream Country is real, which means your subconscious mind knows it, too. When you sleep again, you'll be able to remind yourself to stay safe, to come back. If you're worried about possession—which is extremely rare, by the way—you can draw a circle of salt around your bed before you go to sleep."

Claire looked down at Autumn's palm again and traced the lines with the tip of one finger, frowning in concentration.

"What worries me is, you have two powerful people in your life—both men—who are cosmic opposites, and they are extremely strong. I picture them as a god and a demon, each one pulling at you in opposite directions. Do you know who I mean?"

Autumn took a deep breath. "I think one would be a man I'm seeing. The other would be my father."

Tana shot her a look, and Autumn shook her head slightly to show she was okay.

"Can I speak freely, or would you rather continue our session in private?" Claire asked.

"No, it's alright. Tana and Sylvia are like family, I don't mind if they hear."

"Your father...he created so much damage when you were young that it affected your lines. I see the trauma in your palm. That, too, is very rare. Unfortunately, he's not finished."

"What do you mean?" Autumn asked, sitting up straighter.

"You haven't seen him in a while, correct?"

"At least a decade," Autumn said, "Although we live in the same town."

"I know deep down, you understand you're not free of him, even though you tell yourself often you are. There's always been the possibility he'd come back into your life. I think it will be very soon, and I think the other man will be involved in some way."

Tears welled up in Autumn's eyes and she swallowed again, closing her eyes against the words. This was exactly what she didn't want to hear.

"He'll be involved," Autumn repeated, seeing Killian's face in her mind's eye. "Does that mean he's a bad person?"

"Not at all," Claire said. "I think he has inherent goodness in him. But he's also constantly changing. Not volatile, but—shifting. Adapting. Not a danger to you, but perhaps a liability in some way that might not make sense to you now."

Autumn nodded, trying hard to retain what Claire was saying. The relief she felt at learning Killian was a good guy flooded everything else and made it difficult to listen.

Claire bent over her palm once more, turning it gently in the light. "I see you were taken as a child."

Autumn frowned. "What? Taken how?"

"Kidnapped," Claire said, looking up at her in surprise. "It's right here in the lines. See? This one deviates from the path, marking the time you spent away from your family. About a month, maybe more?"

"Autumn?" Tana said softly, looking at her friend for confirmation.

"I don't know what you're talking about," Autumn said honestly, shaking her head. "I swear."

"You don't remember," said Claire slowly. "You've blocked it out. But maybe you dream about the one who took you."

The bald man suddenly reared into Autumn's mind and she physically recoiled, yanking her hand from Claire's in the process. Had that skeletal horror kidnapped her? Given her a doll and warned it was watching to keep her in line? If so, how had she gotten back home? And why did no one ever mention it again?

Tana moved beside Autumn on the couch and pulled her close, wrapping an arm around her shoulders.

"Do you want to stop?" she whispered.

Autumn wiped her eyes and took a breath. "I'm sorry, Claire, I appreciate the reading, but maybe it would be best to stop here."

"Of course," Claire said, immediately sitting back in her chair. "I'm sorry, I should have warned you; sometimes these readings can go too deep and hit a nerve. Are you alright?"

"I'm fine. I think I need some air, though."

She stood up and walked to the sliding glass door, stepping out into the cold lakeside evening. Tana followed and closed the door behind them, wrapping her arms around herself to stay warm.

"What the hell?" she whispered. "Do you have any memory of that?"

"I didn't until she said that maybe I've been dreaming of the person who took me," Autumn said. "The bald man."

Tana sucked in a breath. "Jesus Christ, Autumn."

"I don't like this," Autumn said. "This whole thing about Killian and my father warring over me, trying to pull me in two different directions. What does that even mean?"

"Maybe that your father created such trauma and chaos in your life, and now Killian is taking you the opposite way. It could be a good thing."

"Yeah, but she said that Killian is going to be involved somehow with my father coming back into my life. I don't want Killian anywhere near him."

Tana put an arm around her and squeezed. "It's going to be okay. Killian is a strong guy. He can handle anything your dad throws at him if it comes to that."

Autumn looked out over the lake, which was a seething mass of dark and choppy waves, and tried to tell herself she agreed.

It was an impossible task.

***

Once Autumn took a few deep breaths outside, she was able to go back in and sit with the others. Tana poured her a finger of whiskey and she sipped as everyone kept the conversation light,

comparing recent movies and books. By eleven o'clock, the group was blurry and tired, and Sylvia insisted that Claire stay the night rather than drive home in the dark.

"Tomorrow we're going to get a fire going in the pit outside and decorate for fall," Sylvia said as they moved toward the stairs. "And I promise, you've never had better sleep than the sleep you get tonight. Fall air by the lake is wonderful for that."

Claire stopped by the room that Tana and Autumn shared after they'd changed into their pajamas.

"I just wanted to say goodnight, and I'm so sorry again for upsetting you," she said to Autumn. "It's not always like that."

"No, please don't be sorry," Autumn said. "I'm sorry for overreacting. I do appreciate the reading. Despite how it may have seemed, you gave me some peace of mind."

"I'm glad," Claire said. "See you in the morning."

Autumn turned out the lights and climbed into one of the twin beds, snuggling beneath the down comforter.

"Your reading was so awesome," she said to Tana. "Can we talk about the fact that you're getting married?"

"I don't know about all that," Tana said with a laugh, but Autumn could tell she was pleased with the idea.

"And you're going to be a mama. A gorgeous, wonderful mama."

"Thanks, babe," Tana said. "I wish your reading had been as positive."

"It's okay. I learned a lot, but I wish my mom was here so I could ask some questions."

"I know, babe," Tana mumbled sleepily. A few moments later, she was snoring lightly.

Autumn rolled over onto her side and looked out the window, where the rain fell steadily against a shadowy moon. Soon she was asleep, falling into the deep place where consciousness slid away and revealed another reality. But this was different, she realized; instead of Dream Country, she was flying over the quarry in the darkness with only the moonlight to guide her.

Suddenly, she snapped awake and sat straight up in bed, heart pounding a tattoo. After a moment, her eyes focused on something bright in the dim room, a white form that seemed to take shape even as she cleared her eyes.

"Brooke?" she asked, her voice wavering with fear.

"Help me, Autumn," Brooke said. Her lower lip trembled, the way it had in the cemetery. "Help me find my mommy."

Chapter Seven

Time seemed to slow. Autumn stared at Brooke for what felt like several minutes, trying to make sense of it. The girl stood there, watching expectantly.

"How did you get here?" Autumn asked in a hoarse whisper. "Brooke, how did you get here?"

She threw the blankets off her legs and walked across the cold, bare floor to where Brooke stood, bending down to look her in the eye.

"I don't know," Brooke said. "I can't remember. I can't find my mom. I want to go home."

She began to cry, face crumpling pitifully as she reached out to Autumn for comfort. Autumn wrapped her arms around the girl...and fell forward, nearly bashing her head on the wall.

Brooke was gone.

Autumn gasped and sat back hard on her butt, looking around her wildly. Brooke had disappeared.

"Tana," Autumn cried, crawling for a moment on her hands and knees toward Tana's bed. "Tana, wake up."

"Hmm?" Tana mumbled.

Autumn shook Tana's shoulder roughly, the full effect of her shock and fear exploding into her veins.

"Tana, I think Brooke is dead. Please wake up," Autumn begged.

"What?" Tana sat up in bed and grabbed Autumn's forearms, trying to steady her. "What are you talking about?"

"She was here, she said she was lost and then she disappeared, she was a ghost. Oh my god, Tana, Brooke is dead," Autumn said, gulping for air.

"Hold on," Tana said, standing up to be eye-to-eye with her friend. "Take a deep breath. Take another one. Slow down, and start over."

Autumn breathed in through her nose and exhaled slowly and shakily, trying to will herself not to be violently ill. She sat on the edge of Tana's bed and bent over at the waist in an attempt to calm herself.

"I woke up and Brooke was standing over there," she said finally, pointing to the corner. "I asked her how she got here, and she said she didn't remember. She said she was lost, that she needed my help finding her mom."

Tana sat beside her. "Babe, you were dreaming. I'm sure…"

Autumn shook her head. "No, no, you don't understand. I was awake, I know I was. She started crying and I moved to hug her, to comfort her, and she disappeared like smoke. I have to call Rose."

She jumped up and grabbed her phone from the nightstand.

"Autumn, wait," Tana cried. "It's three in the morning. You're going to scare that poor woman half to death over a dream."

"I don't care, I have to know," Autumn said.

Rose's phone rang once, twice, three times. On the fourth ring, she picked up blearily. "Hello?" she mumbled.

"Rose? It's Autumn. I'm sorry to call so late but I need you to check on Brooke."

"What?" More alert to Autumn's great relief. "What do you mean? What's wrong?"

"Please, I'll explain in a minute, just go check on her right now."

She heard the clunk of the phone being dropped, rustling on the line as Rose got out of bed. There were unintelligible murmurs in the background for a few moments and then Rose returned, out of breath.

"She's fine," she said, and Autumn felt her knees give out. Fortunately, the bed was there to catch her fall. "She was asleep, breathing normally. I tried to wake her up, but she was in too deep like she has been lately."

"Oh thank god," Autumn said.

"What the hell is this about?" Rose asked, irritation edging her voice. "Why are you calling me at three in the morning to check on my sleeping daughter?"

"I'm so sorry, Rose," Autumn said. "I guess I had a bad dream. I thought it was real for a minute. Thank you so much for checking."

"Yeah, well. I know somethin' about bad dreams," Rose said, softer. "Go back to bed. Tomorrow will look better."

Autumn thanked her and hung up, dissolving into tears. Tana sat down beside her again and began rubbing her back in slow, comforting circles.

"Are you okay?"

"I don't know, Tana, I really don't," Autumn said thickly. "What the hell is wrong with me?"

"Nothing," Tana said firmly. "You had a palm reading that understandably freaked you out, you've had a lot on your mind, and your subconscious slapped all that together and created something that felt real. That's all."

"I feel like I'm losing my mind. It was as real as you and me, sitting here talking."

"The worst dreams are," Tana said. "And thanks to Claire, we know that you're a vivid dreamer by nature. Stress or anxiety probably only make it worse."

"Yeah. I guess so."

"Listen, tomorrow we're going to have a fun day, and we're not going to think about any of this, okay? Why don't you get back into bed and think about your man? Picture that handsome face and that tight butt. That'll help you have good dreams."

Autumn laughed despite herself and nodded, swiping at her eyes. "Okay. Thanks, Tan."

She climbed back into her bed and pulled the blankets up to her chin, turning to see the moon through the window. An old maple tree rattled against the glass pane like dry bones in a coffin. She closed her eyes and pictured Killian, pushing everything else out forcefully.

Eventually, she slept.

***

In the light of morning, Autumn's vision of Brooke seemed more like a dream than it had in the dark. She dressed quickly after waking late and joined Tana and her parents downstairs to find Claire had already left.

"She asked me to give this to you," Sylvia said at the breakfast table, passing Autumn a business card. "Said to tell you that if you have any questions or want another reading, you can feel free to call her. She was very impressed with you."

"I was afraid she thought I was rude," Autumn said, turning the card over in her hand. On the back, in a rounded script, Claire had written *Embrace your abilities*.

"Not at all," said Sylvia. "She said you were one of the most interesting people she's met in a while."

"That's got to be a compliment coming from someone like her," Greg said with a laugh, refilling Tana's cup and pouring some coffee for Autumn.

Tana was trying to catch Autumn's gaze over her cup, her dark eyes asking, *You okay?*

Autumn nodded and smiled, despite the underlying worry she was losing her mind.

The thought nagged at her throughout the morning and into the afternoon as she helped Tana and Sylvia stack pumpkins on the front porch, hang wreaths, and set up fall-themed tableaus on the mantels and kitchen table. By the time dinner was over and their bags were packed, Autumn was more than ready to go home and take a hot bath in a comfortable, familiar setting. Her anxiety was dialed up, compounded by the feeling that her mental health was declining and the fear that her experience from the night before was a warning of some kind.

"You're not crazy," Tana said as she drove down the darkened roads leading home. "You've been stressed, your sleep schedule is all messed up, and according to an expert in the supernatural, you fucking *travel* while you dream. Leaving your body has to take a toll on your mind at some point, no?"

"So you believe what she said?" Autumn asked.

"I believe in possibilities," said Tana. "Who am I to declare something is wrong just because I've never experienced it myself?"

"I appreciate your open-mindedness, but if this was happening to you...would you be freaked out?"

"Sure. But you'd have my back, right?"

"Of course."

"Well, there you go. I'm not going to let anything bad happen to you."

Autumn laughed. "That's sweet, but you can't control it any more than I can. What happens when I dream....sometimes it feels real and sometimes I know it's not. I can't always tell the difference. Let's say this astral projection thing is actual. What if something happens to me out in the world while my sleeping body is lying prone in bed? What if I can't get back?"

Tana was quiet for a long moment. "I don't know. Maybe you should call Claire when you get home. She said to get in touch if you had questions."

"Yeah. Maybe. I don't know, maybe I need a good night of proper sleep."

They were approaching Autumn's house. Tana pulled up in front and parked but left the engine running.

"You want me to come in with you, help you get settled?"

Autumn smiled. "No, but thank you. Once again, you have to step into the role of my parent. I'm sorry, Tan. I appreciate you taking me with you this weekend. I did have a good time, despite what it may have seemed like."

"I'll be your parent anytime," Tana said. "Go inside and get some rest. Flick the porch light on so I know you're okay."

She waited at the curb until Autumn unlocked the door and switched on the light, and then she was gone in the dark. Autumn dropped her bags and lit the lamp closest to her in the living room, then froze.

The room was trashed.

Books, papers, candles, and pillows lay on the floor; her couch had been slashed, and stuffing lay in little piles everywhere. Plants had been unpotted, dirt scattered on the hardwood floor along with broken leaves. The chill coming from upstairs told her at least one window was broken. She walked gingerly through the living room and into the kitchen, turning on lights as she went. The destruction was complete. Dishes were smashed, the tea kettle lay overturned and leaking onto the counter, and the refrigerator had been emptied of its contents. The door lay open, spilling sad yellow light onto the floor alongside broken jelly jars and condiment bottles.

Nothing appeared to have been taken. Autumn collapsed into a chair, fury rising up like a wave. There were only two people who hated her enough to trash her home but not steal a thing.

She rummaged through her pockets and found her phone.

***

David stood in the middle of the living room, hands on his hips, surveying the destruction.

"Christ, Autumn," he said softly. "Is there anything they didn't damage?"

"The upstairs bathroom isn't too bad," Autumn said humorlessly. She stood by the window looking out onto the street, wishing she had a cigarette for the first time in years. "They ripped down the shower curtain. Also, I notice you said "they", meaning you know who did this the same as I do."

David shook his head. "We can't know that for sure. Could'a been kids, broke in while you were gone an' had a little party. Teenagers are so bored in this town they'd probably trade their own mothers for a movie theater."

"This wasn't kids and you know it," Autumn said between clenched teeth. Between her experiences at the lake house and this, she was the most on edge she'd been in a while. "Now I want to know what you're going to do about it."

"I can't go off half-cocked, accusing someone of a crime, if I don't have any evidence. There're no prints on the doors or windows other than yours. What I *can* do is ask your neighbors if they have surveillance cameras, or if any of them saw anyone during the time you were gone."

"That's it?"

"Autumn, I know this is frustrating. I'm real sorry your stuff got destroyed, but the most I can do is file a report for now. And I promise you, if I do find out the Napiers had anything to do with this, I'll toss their butts in jail quicker than they can say "Boo"."

Autumn watched him go, silently seething. The Napiers were untouchable and they knew it. Nothing was ever going to change, and it frustrated her beyond measure.

She went into the kitchen to begin the cleanup process but was interrupted by a knock on the front door. It was Killian, worriedly peering through the glass. She pulled open the door and flew into his arms, so filled with relief at his return that she couldn't even speak.

"Hey, is everything okay?" he asked, wrapping his arms around her. "I passed the Chief as he was leaving."

Just as he finished his sentence, he realized the living room was in shambles and sucked in a breath, scanning the damage through narrowed eyes.

"What the hell happened?"

"I went out of town yesterday, to Tana's family's lake house. When I got back a little while ago, I found all this waiting for me."

Killian released her and walked slowly through the room, inspecting the ruination of her life with a growing frown on his handsome face. She could feel his anger building and walked toward him with a sigh.

"How was your trip? Successful?" she asked.

"I don't know if I'd call it that," he said, running a hand through his hair. "But it wasn't entirely a waste. Listen, what did the Chief say about all this?"

Autumn rolled her eyes. "It's pretty clear this was the Napiers, but he doesn't want to say it out loud. I guess I can't blame him. They can pull some strings and have the county investigate his job performance or worse if they get a mind to. Anyway, they didn't leave any trace of themselves behind, so there's no physical evidence to tie them to it, and they didn't steal anything. They were smart. Worse they'd get slapped with is breaking and entering and destruction of property, but those wouldn't even carry much weight. Not for guys like them."

Killian's jaw set. "Well, that's a bunch of bullshit. What can I do to help?"

She wrapped her arms around his waist, suddenly so glad to have him there that the destruction of her inner sanctum seemed distant and unimportant.

"Not a thing right now, except maybe hug me," she said softly, tilting her chin to look up at him.

"I can do better than that," he said and dipped to kiss her.

He tasted sweet, his lips warm and soft. His hands slid over her hips and she leaned into him, wanting more. He rewarded her by moving his mouth lower, placing kisses along the line of her jaw and down her throat. Suddenly it felt like time was moving too slow and she couldn't stand it anymore. Her fingers caught the hem of his shirt and yanked it up so she could run her hands over his stomach and chest; after a moment she pulled it over his head and tossed it to the floor.

He returned the favor, lifting her t-shirt slowly and skimming his fingertips over her ribcage. When she was standing before him in only her bra and jeans, he pulled away to look at her.

"My god," he said softly. "You are so beautiful. Look at your skin. Soft and perfect."

She shook her head. "You're the beautiful one."

When he pulled her to him once more she slithered out of his grasp and knelt before him, mindful of the detritus on the floor, looking up to meet his eyes as she unbuttoned his jeans. She caught a glimpse of soft, blue cotton boxer briefs before he hauled her up by her forearms.

"Don't," he said. "I'll lose control, and I don't want to hurt you."

She studied his eyes. "You wouldn't hurt me."

She stepped back and undid her bra, letting it fall to the floor. When she pushed her jeans down and slid out of them, revealing a black thong, he sucked in a breath and wrapped his big hands around her waist, picking her up so he could take her mouth again. Glass and splintered wood crunched beneath his boots as he moved across the floor. She crossed her long legs around

his hips and held on tight, running her fingers through his hair as his tongue found hers. When he moved toward the stairs, she pulled away and shook her head.

"I can't wait for that," she moaned. "Do it here."

He made a sound deep in his throat and sat her gently on one of the stair treads, kneeling between her legs. She watched as he hooked his fingers beneath the waistband of her panties and slowly pulled them down, a purposeful tease. She lifted her bottom to make it easier and he tossed the underwear aside, focusing his attention on her bare thighs and the soft skin that awaited him.

She spread her knees apart to give him access to the most secret part of her and he obliged, cupping her ass with both hands and flicking his tongue over her clit. She gasped and placed her hands on either side of his head, holding him there. It was unnecessary; he wasn't going anywhere. He sucked and swirled, using his tongue and lips to bring her to the edge before pulling away and dropping soft kisses on her inner thighs. When he finally made his way back to where she wanted him, he parted her with his tongue, sliding open the soft seam and licking upward before pulling her clit between his lips and sucking more firmly than he had before, working her into a frenzy. Her legs trembled, and she leaned against the stairs, arching her back and bucking her hips up against his mouth as she came. He kept his mouth on her, licking her clean as she spiraled down slowly; it seemed to take an eternity.

Before she could catch her breath, Killian slid his arms beneath her back and under her legs, picking her up so he could carry her upstairs. She rested her head against him, feeling the sort of safety she had always wished for but never had. Her legs were still weak when he entered the bedroom and sat her on the bed. She leaned back on her hands and watched as he began to undress, pushing down his jeans and kicking them out of the way. Before he could go further, she looked up at him and placed a gentle hand on the hard bulge straining against cotton. He watched her for a moment and then closed his eyes, clearly trying to maintain control.

"Is this okay?" she asked softly.

He nodded, breathing heavily through his nose. Her hand moved down, then back up, measuring the size of him; he was massive. *No wonder he was afraid of hurting me*, she thought in wonder. Not just big, but incredibly hard. She leaned forward and put her mouth on him over his underwear, feeling his body tense up in response. When she breathed against him, he moaned and slid his hands into her hair.

"Oh, Autumn," he said, his voice deeper than she'd ever heard it. "You're gonna be the death of me."

She smiled up at him and slid his underwear down, watching delightedly as his cock sprang out. She took as much of him into her mouth as she could, grasping firmly at the base, and he groaned loudly. Spurred on, she slid her lips down and sucked firmly as she came back up, drawing him to her like a magnet.

"Stop," he said through clenched teeth. "Please, stop."

She pulled away immediately and looked up. "What's wrong?"

"Nothing, except that I'm about to explode and I'm not ready to do that yet," he said, helping her up from the floor.

He placed one hand gently at the small of her back and laid her on the bed, moving over her at the same time. She saw he'd procured a condom from somewhere and was sliding it on as he met her eyes.

"If it's too much, or if I go too hard, you say something immediately. Okay?" he asked.

She nodded, not caring if it hurt. She wanted him so badly there was a literal ache between her legs, a deep throbbing that wouldn't be satisfied until she felt him inside her. When he began slowly pushing forward, she parted her thighs and took him in, arching her back to offer all of herself to him. He groaned softly and pushed himself a little deeper, watching her the entire time to make sure she was okay.

Autumn sighed and closed her eyes, focusing on the weight of him and the way he moved with such satisfaction on his face, seeming to savor every inch of her. She grabbed his ass and pulled him forward, pushing him deeper inside her with every thrust. He made a rumbling sound that was part ecstasy, part loss of control. He dipped his head, brushed her nipples with his tongue, the bristle of his beard leaving a delicious trail of fire across her skin.

Suddenly he rolled, pulling her with him. He ended sitting up in bed and holding her on his lap without ever leaving her, and she gasped at his strength. Facing him, her legs wrapped around his waist, she was in control. It was exactly what she needed. She rearranged herself and put her knees on the bed, leaning over him, her breasts level with his mouth. He gave all his attention to her nipples, licking and sucking and teasing, and she lifted herself so he slid out of her for a moment. When he looked at her questioningly, she reached behind herself and wrapped a hand around the base of his cock, guiding him back inside slowly. Torturing him. His mouth fell open and a great roar of ecstasy escaped him as he wrapped his arms around her waist and held her tight. She contracted her muscles around him, moving faster, taking more of him in with every stroke, and when she felt the waves building in him she found his mouth and covered it with hers, muffling his cries of pleasure.

He shuddered into her, triggering her orgasm, and she rode him harder as it tumbled through her body unchecked. With her arms thrown around his neck, she leaned back and shouted toward the ceiling.

Slowly, slowly, they coasted down, both panting. Rather than loosening his grip on her, he pulled her closer and kissed her collarbone, her jaw, her lips, her cheek. She looked into his dark eyes and smiled.

"I want more," she whispered.

***

When morning came, Autumn and Killian lay exhausted in each other's arms.

She rested her head on his chest and looked up at him, still hardly able to believe the night they'd spent together. It had been better than she'd dared to hope for, and she was amazed at their ability to keep going, over and over again. It was the connection that did it, the spark that turned into a buzzing electricity every time they touched each other and left them wanting more rather than supplying satisfaction.

As a fall breeze fluttered her curtains through the broken window, she touched his face.

"Are you awake?" she asked softly and was rewarded with a deep rumble.

"Only halfway," came his answer, and she smiled. "What time is it?"

"Seven. Think I could get away with calling in sick, or would Tana see right through me?"

"I don't think anyone could get away with much when Tana's involved," Killian said.

"Yeah, she's a tough cookie," Autumn said, stretching. "Way tougher than me."

He pulled her close and touched her cheek gently. "You're much tougher than you give yourself credit for."

Parting was incredibly difficult but Autumn needed a shower. For a moment, she thought about asking him to join her but knew if she did, she'd never make it into work. Her heart sank again when she realized the state of her bathroom. Killian managed to fix the shower curtain for her, although it hung crookedly where it was torn.

"What's the plan for cleaning up?" he asked. "I can help."

Autumn brushed out her long hair and pulled it back with a tortoiseshell clip, her head spinning with the events of the past few days. She inwardly groaned at the thought of all the work that awaited her.

"I don't know. I'll have to call someone to come and replace the windows, which will probably take a couple of days. I'll get started with the cleanup tonight, I don't have time to do much right now. You can stay as long as you like after I leave, though. What do you have planned for today? Still on the hunt for this mystery person?"

She'd meant for it to come across lightly, but there was an edge to her voice that even she didn't understand and which registered on Killian's face immediately. Was she irritated beneath the surface because he still hadn't confided in her about why he was really in Pine Hollow? She didn't understand why it should be so important to her.

"Yeah," he said evenly. "I think I'm close."

"I meant what I said about helping you," Autumn said. "If you'd tell me what you're looking for—"

"That's the thing," he interrupted. "I can't explain what I'm looking for. It's not as simple as black-and-white, it's not something you can look up on the internet. I'm sorry I can't be clearer than that."

She turned into him, wrapping her arms as far around his body as they would go. "I'm sorry, I promise I'm not trying to pry. I want to help if I can. I'm worried about you."

He pulled back and tilted her chin up. "Why should you be worried about me?"

"I don't know," she said, suddenly feeling emotional. Tears burned the back of her throat and she swallowed them down. "You said what you're doing might be dangerous and that scares me. I don't want you to get hurt."

"I'm not going to get hurt." His voice was pitched low and deep, at the level that formed shivers inside her. "I'm going to do the hurting."

***

Somehow, Autumn made it to the office before Tana did, a rare occasion. She brewed a pot of tea and nursed it at her desk, going through her calendar for the week while she waited. It would be a busy one, and she tried to gather enough strength to face it head-on, suddenly feeling more exhausted than she ever had. Of course, her sleep schedule had been erratic for the past few days. What she needed was a solid night of rest.

"Morning," Tana said as she swept in, wearing a fashionably knotted red scarf that popped against the gloom of the day. "How are you feeling?"

Autumn smiled. "Well, that's a complicated question with an even more complicated answer."

"Why? Did something happen?" Tana asked, setting her purse down on her desk.

"Yes. Something happened all night long," Autumn said with a yawn. "I'm exhausted."

"Oh my god," said Tana. "Oh my GOD. You did it? How was it? How was he? How do you feel?"

"It was mind-blowing. He was incredibly perfect. And I feel like shit because between all the sex and my house getting trashed, I got very little sleep."

Tana pulled her chair over to Autumn's desk and sat down to face her. "What do you mean? Trashed from all the sex? How wild is this guy?"

Autumn hadn't imagined she would ever find what had happened funny, but she laughed anyway and shook her head. It was too much on top of everything else.

"No, although there was a moment on the stairs…" she began, and Tana's eyes widened. "But I'm getting ahead of myself. When I got inside last night, my place was wrecked. Someone...or *two someones,* I would imagine...broke in and destroyed a bunch of stuff, smashed windows and mirrors, basically sent me a message they can do whatever they want to me."

"What the hell?" Tana said, straightening up in her chair. "Why didn't you call me? I would have come right back."

Autumn waved a hand at her. "It's fine. I called David and he came over, saw the mess, and dusted for fingerprints, which were nonexistent. They knew what they were doing."

"The Napiers," Tana said through clenched teeth.

"Bingo. I don't think they took anything, just trashed the place."

"So what did David say?"

"Basically his hands are tied. He's got no physical proof it was them."

"But that's bullshit," Tana cried.

"I know, but I understand his side, too," Autumn said. "They'd make his life a living hell if he even thought about bringing them in for questioning without evidence."

"But they attacked you at the cemetery. He's got probable cause."

"It's okay. I'm going to go home tonight and clean up and keep my distance from the Napiers, and if they make a move against me again I'll be ready. I'm calling a security company today about a surveillance system."

Tana settled back into her chair. "Well, that's a relief, at least. Listen, I want you to wait for me every day so we can walk in and out together. No going out for lunch by yourself anymore, I'll go with you."

"I don't want you to completely rearrange your life for me—"

"I'm not rearranging my life," Tana interrupted. "I'm doing what's necessary. This is serious. I'm not going to give those two assholes any more opportunities to get at you. What did Killian say about it?"

"He wasn't happy," Autumn said, slowly stirring honey into her tea. She was so tired that the world around her had become dreamlike, misty. She thought back to the previous night and recalled Killian's stealthy anger, and what he'd said that morning before she left: *I'm going to do the hurting.* What was he capable of? It unsettled her that she'd gotten so involved with him before she knew the answer.

The morning flew by quickly as Autumn struggled to keep up with emails and phone appointments in her tired state. When her cell phone rang at lunchtime, she answered without even looking at the caller ID. It was Rose.

"Brooke has been upset this morning," Rose said. She sounded tired, more than usual. "She wants to talk to you. Think you could come by today?"

"Yes," Autumn said, startled. In the wake of all that had happened, she'd all but forgotten about her dream of ghost-Brooke and what it might mean. "I'll be there in an hour."

***

When Autumn pulled up, Brooke was playing with her dolls in the front yard, Rose keeping watch from the front porch. Autumn waved to her and she nodded, her face a pale and impassive mask beneath the scarf she'd wrapped around her head. Chemotherapy treatments left her feeling sick and thinned her hair, something Autumn knew Rose hated. She didn't want Brooke's last memories of her to be tainted with illness.

"Hey, you," Autumn said as she closed her car door.

Brook dropped her dolls immediately and ran to her for a tight hug.

"You came," she cried.

"Of course I came, I always come," Autumn said with a smile. "How are you today?"

The little girl's face fell and she turned to Rose, who nodded gentle encouragement.

"I had a real bad dream about you," Brooke said. She wasn't crying, but she was close; a hiccup escaped her as she tried to rein in her emotions. "I was looking for my mom in the woods but she wasn't there, and then I found you in a house but you couldn't help me. You disappeared, like in a cartoon. And then I was flying over the water and I was all alone."

Autumn studied her for a moment. "That sounds like a scary dream, alright. What happened when you woke up?"

Brooke shrugged. "I can't remember. I was glad to be in my bed. But I wanted to tell you about the roses."

"What roses?"

The little girl frowned, searching the ground as she tried to recall her dream in its entirety. "I can't remember. I just know it's important. Stay away from the roses."

"Would you like to go for a walk with me?" Autumn asked, looking up at Rose for confirmation that it was okay. She nodded and Autumn took Brooke's hand. "Come on, I'll tell you about some of my crazy dreams. Then yours won't seem so bad."

They walked around the expansive property, their feet *shushing* through fallen leaves, as Autumn relayed some of her silliest dreams. They talked about what it meant to dream about flying, what symbolism was, and how to focus before bedtime to try and keep nightmares at bay.

"No matter what happens," Autumn said, "You have to remember dreams can't hurt you. They're like movies that play in your mind. Sometimes your brain gets confused and slips in something that seems scary by accident, but it's just a mistake. Everyone makes mistakes sometimes, right?"

"Yeah, like Uncle Bill's dogs pooping everywhere," Brooke said, making a face.

"Exactly," Autumn said with a laugh. "You're a very smart person, Brooke, and sometimes smart people's brains work overtime. That means your dreams can feel real, but they're rather like mini-movies."

"I'd rather watch *Matilda*," Brooke said, and Autumn laughed again.

Back at the house, Brooke went back to her dolls while Autumn talked with Rose.

"Thanks for coming out," Rose said. "She was agitated all morning until I called you. Said it was important."

"She's okay now, I think," Autumn said. "I had vivid dreams as a kid, too. I remember how hard it was to keep telling myself they weren't real. We talked about ways she can relax before bedtime to try and keep the nightmares away, but I can type up a list and email it to you if you'd like."

"That'd be nice, thank you," Rose said gratefully. "She's never been a good sleeper, since she was a baby. But it's only gotten worse since Tommy died."

"She's been through a lot. It's to be expected. But the good news is that there are things you can do to help her. And if you need anything at all, you can call me, day or night."

"I appreciate that. She loves you, you know."

"I love her, too. She's a great kid. And I'm so sorry for calling you the other night," Autumn said. Before she could explain, the apology slammed the memory of her dream into her mind and she physically recoiled from it, putting a hand to her head.

I found you in a house, but you couldn't help me, Brooke had said. *You disappeared, like in a cartoon.*

Autumn let out a shaky breath. "Rose, that dream of Brooke's...did she have it last night?"

"No, Saturday night," Rose said, frowning in concentration. "She didn't mention it until yesterday morning, but I didn't want to call you on a Sunday and interrupt your day."

Chapter Eight

By the time Autumn returned home, she was so weary and consumed with her thoughts that at first she didn't even see all the changes that had taken place while she was at work.

Stepping inside the house, she realized that cardboard had been duct-taped to the windows and the living room floor was spotless. Tables had been righted, books had been replaced, shelves had been re-hung. The kitchen was sparkling clean, and there was a note on the table scrawled in Killian's spiky cursive:

Went to pick up some dinner. Lock the doors behind you. Back soon.

She hadn't given him a key. He must have locked up and gone for food assuming that she would be home before him. Autumn smiled and pocketed the note, briefly forgetting the strangeness of the day as gratitude warmed her up. It had been years since anyone had been so thoughtful. She had given up hope long ago that a man would come along who loved her enough to be selfless, yet here he was. Too good to be true.

That stilled the smile on her lips. Too good to be true, so where did that leave her? Falling hard for a man who did all the right things but couldn't be straightforward with her. That old protective shield began to form around her heart, the one she'd built after the last relationship took too much from her.

She was too tired to think in circles. When Killian returned laden with takeout bags, she smiled up at him and simply allowed herself to enjoy the moment, wrapping her arms around his waist in a fierce hug.

"You shouldn't have done all this," she said, gesturing to the house. "It's too much."

"It was nothing. Took me half an hour," he said, dropping the bags on the table so he could return her hug. "I hope it's okay I did it without you. I realized after I was finished it might seem like an intrusion, but I didn't want to go off and leave those broken windows untouched."

"I figured if a thief came by he'd see the mess and turn back around," she joked. "Seriously, I appreciate all this. You have no idea. I've been so tired all day, and the thought of cleaning all this up made me seriously entertain the idea of getting a hotel room."

"I'm sorry I kept you up all night," he said, leaning down to kiss her earlobe. "That was pretty rude of me."

She felt the melting begin in the pit of her stomach and let her body go slack in his arms; he was holding her up with barely any effort.

"So rude," she said, lifting the hem of his shirt to run her fingertips along his warm skin. "I think you're going to have to find a way to make it up to me."

"Oh, I will," he said, "But first, you need to eat something. You need to keep your energy up, and I brought fried chicken from Gertie's."

Autumn hadn't thought it possible only moments before, but at the mention of food her entire body perked up. They sat at the kitchen table and dug in, and she realized that in all the commotion of the day, she'd forgotten to eat lunch.

"This is amazing," she said around a mouthful of buttery biscuit. "You keep saving me today."

"Hey, I just took your tip and ran with it. Remember? You told me about Gertie's that first night when we were walking around town."

She smiled. "Of course. I remember everything about that night in startling detail."

"Oh yeah? I wish I did. Mostly what I remember is looking at you and not being able to look at anything else."

Autumn felt heat rise to her cheeks and looked down at the table, but he lifted her chin gently to meet his gaze.

"You always do that," he said.

"Do what?" she asked, eyes wide.

"You look away when I tell you how beautiful you are. Does it embarrass you?"

"I'm not sure how to respond," she said, choosing her words carefully. The exhaustion that had relented earlier was back with a vengeance. "No one has ever said that to me before."

Killian smiled, a confused look in his eyes. "You're kidding. Right?"

She shook her head. "When I was little, my father's nickname for me was "Ugly Duckling". The relationships I've had—none of them used the word *beautiful* to describe me. *Cute*, once or twice. Never beautiful."

Autumn had been looking at her hands as she spoke. When she looked back up at him, she saw a mixture of sadness and indignation on his face. Anger furrowed his brow as he took her hands across the table.

"I can see this is something I'm not going to be able to fix by saying some words," he said. "It's been ground into you by assholes with ugly hearts who probably thought if they built you up, you'd realize what utter fucking losers they were. You're not ugly, Autumn. You've never been. You shine, and I'm going to help you unlearn what you've been told."

She didn't realize she was crying until he reached out and wiped a tear from her cheek. When he pulled away and stood up, extending a hand to her, she let him help her up and into his arms.

"Why are you so kind to me?" she asked.

"Because you deserve it," he said.

She rubbed her eyes, feeling more tired than she ever had before now that her belly was full, and felt his hand on her cheek. His fingers slid down her throat and came back up, hesitating at the corner of her mouth. For a moment, she smelled his unique scent over the food smells in the kitchen, something warm, reminding her of smoke in the forest. When his thumb slid across her bottom lip she opened her mouth and took it in, sucking it gently, raising her eyes to his. It was what she wanted now, to be held and kissed and fucked so hard she could finally stop thinking. She released him and stood up, shucking her t-shirt and letting it fall into his lap as she walked by.

In her bed, she let him pull her panties down over her hips, his dark hair tickling her thighs as he teased her with his tongue. She bucked her hips up against him and grabbed his shoulders to pull him up, wanting his cock so bad she felt a moan bubble up in her throat. He slid up and into her, incredibly hard and hot. She contracted around him and watched his face, his eyes closed against the pleasure.

And later, the desire was still there, but it had changed. Seeing how tired she was, he pulled the comforter back and slid into bed with her, holding her against his warm chest so she could have a measure of comfort while she slept. Autumn immediately felt relaxed, but something nagged at her, something she wished she could share with Killian but was afraid to. *How can I tell him?* she thought. *He'll think I'm crazy.*

As she spiraled toward unconsciousness, Autumn cast her mind out toward Brooke, hoping against hope that they would find one another on the right plane.

Because she was sure Brooke was a traveler, just like she was.

***

In the darkness, there was only the sound of Autumn's breathing. Slow and steady, a sound like distant waves on a shore.

She opened her eyes and found herself standing in the trees beneath a bright moon. Up ahead, the opening to the quarry awaited her like a giant mouth. She walked forward with care, but there was no need. The pine needles underfoot were as soft as cotton.

The crackle of a broken branch whipped her head around and she crouched, afraid of being seen. After a moment she spied something pale bobbing through the bushes to her right.

"Brooke?" she whispered.

Silence, then: "Autumn?"

Autumn straightened up and held her arms out, unable to contain a relieved laugh as Brooke emerged from the greenery. The little girl hugged her fiercely.

"I found you," Brooke said.

"You sure did," Autumn said. She pulled away and knelt to look Brooke in the eyes. "Do you remember how you found me?"

Brooke shrugged. "I closed my eyes and thought about where you were, and I saw trees. Big trees, so I knew they weren't the ones around my house. And then I heard you say my name."

So Brooke had truly found her, it seemed. Autumn had cast her mind out to locate the girl, but all she'd managed to do was find a place Brooke would recognize. After that, she'd drawn Brooke to her like a magnet. The thought was both incredibly exciting and terrifying at the same time. What sort of trouble could a seven-year-old get into while traveling outside of her own body? Autumn shuddered at the idea as a thousand thoughts ran through her head. How

could she keep Brooke safe if she couldn't keep her from projecting onto another plane of existence?

"Brooke, how often do you do this? Think about someone so you can find them, I mean."

"All the time," she said with a shrug. "One time my cat ran away, and when I went to bed that night I thought real hard about where he was and I found him trapped inside the neighbor's shed."

"And when you woke up, you went to the shed and rescued him?"

Brooke gave her a confused look. "No, I saved him that night and took him home."

Autumn frowned as she recalled the night Brooke had appeared to her at the lake house. So it was true. Not only could Brooke travel in her sleep, but she could also manipulate the real world when she did it, and that was huge. Thinking back on her own experiences, Autumn realized she'd only ever felt like a visitor when she traveled, an outsider who could do no more than watch the events unfolding before her. The world was insubstantial in that state. She could barely feel the ground beneath her feet. Something about her memories nagged at her, but she couldn't place the worry.

"Brooke, listen. You must try not to do this anymore."

"But why? What if my cat gets loose again?"

"Then you call me and I'll help you find him," Autumn said. "Do you remember what we talked about before? About how dreams are just like little movies that your brain makes up?"

"Yeah…"

"Well, your dreams are special, and so are mine. Sometimes, we can make the movies come to life."

Brooke's eyes widened. "Really?"

"Yes. Right now, our bodies are asleep, but another part of us is awake, here in the woods. I know it's confusing, Bee, but it's not safe for us to be here. It's better if you stay in your bed. Do you remember how to get back to your house?"

"Yes. I have to think about it," Brooke said. "But Autumn…I can't always control where I go. Sometimes I'll have a dream and I know it's a dream because it's silly, like the one where everything looked like a cartoon and there were mountains made out of ice cream. But one time I dreamed about my dad and I went to the cemetery. I wasn't thinking about him before I went to sleep, but I dreamed he was working on his truck in the driveway and then I was standing in the graveyard. It was scary in the dark."

Her lower lip trembled and Autumn pulled her close, wrapping protective arms around her. The little girl had so much weighing on her narrow shoulders, Autumn had no idea how to keep her safe. It sent a bolt of terror through her body.

"I bet that *was* scary," Autumn said, trying to strengthen her voice. "But you know what? I'm here with you, and I'm going to help you. I just met a very smart lady who knows all about these dreams. She calls what we do "traveling", just like when you take a trip in the car. I bet she could help us figure out how to stop. But in the meantime, I want you to try your hardest to stay in bed, every night. If you do travel in a dream, don't stay there. Think about your house right away."

"But what if I can't get back?" Brooke cried, suddenly panicked. The tears that had been threatening began to spill over her dark lashes. "What if I get stuck?"

It was exactly what Autumn was afraid might happen, but she didn't want to scare the girl any more than she already had.

"Then you find me like you did before, exactly like you did tonight," Autumn said, taking her hand and smiling. "You are so strong, Brooke. You're the strongest person I know. You have the power to control this. It might feel scary at first, but we're going to figure out how to fix it together, okay?"

Brooke swiped a hand over her eyes and nodded. "Okay."

"Right now I want you to close your eyes and think about your bed. Picture it in your mind. Do you see it?"

"Yes," she sniffed.

"Go on back to sleep, and I'll come to visit tomorrow. Sound good?"

Brooke nodded and yawned. "See you tomorrow," she mumbled, her body already becoming insubstantial. After a moment, she evaporated like steam into the night air.

Autumn sat and took several long, deep breaths, trying to straighten out her thoughts. There was so much to consider, so much to do; she had to contact Claire, she had to talk to Tana, she had to warn Rose...

Rose. How on earth was she supposed to tell a woman battling cancer that her daughter had the power to leave her body? That doing so might put her in grave danger? Autumn wrapped an arm around her midsection, suddenly feeling as though she might be sick. After several long moments, she stood up, breathed deep, and cast her thoughts toward Killian, who was still lying warm and unconscious in her bed.

***

Autumn woke slowly. It reminded her of swimming as a child, when she'd dive deep into the quarry and find her way to the wavery surface, kicking hard to propel herself upward.

When she finally opened her eyes, she was disoriented. The room was pitch black, with the familiar sound of the ceiling fan whirring above, and after a moment she recognized Killian's breathing next to her. She reached out and lightly touched his arm to feel something real, to tether herself to the world.

"Hmm?" he said softly, turning to wrap his arms around her. She rolled into him and pressed her lips to his neck, inhaling the scent of his sleep-warm skin. Now that she'd had some rest, all she wanted was the strength of him and the feel of his mouth on her body again. When the sun came up, she'd be able to tackle everything else.

"I'm sorry to wake you," she whispered. "I just had a bad dream. Go back to sleep."

She knew he'd do no such thing. His strong arms were around her waist, holding her tightly to him, and the heat of his body radiated against her hips and breasts. His heart was pounding; she put her hand on his bare chest, comforted by the steady beat, and he bent his head to kiss her.

"Don't be sorry," he said when he pulled away. "Are you alright?"

"I'm fine," she whispered, stretching her neck slightly to put her mouth closer to his. Their lips were so close she could feel his breath trembling the air between them. "I'm glad you're here."

His hand slid beneath her shirt and traced her bare skin, making her suck in a breath. His fingertips almost felt electrified as they ran along her side, up the center of her body, and back down. She reached for the waistband of his shorts and he stopped her with a strong hand, bringing her wrist up above her head and pinning it to the mattress.

"Not yet," he growled. He pulled away in the dark and reappeared above her, moving slowly down the bed, undressing her as he did so. When she was completely bare, he kissed a line of fire up the pale skin of her thighs, over the soft curve of her lower belly, across her breasts. She reached out to touch his face, to bring his mouth to hers, and he obliged. Kissing him was like inhaling an intoxicant. Euphoric dizziness struck and she clung to him to keep the world from slipping away from her.

With his lips still on hers, he reached down and stroked her open, fingertips softly massaging the most sensitive part of her. She gasped when he rubbed his thumb against her clit,

creating delicious friction. She moved her hips up, wanting more, but he was determined to tease her as much as possible and kept the pressure light.

"Please," she whimpered against his mouth.

"Please what?" he asked, his voice a deep well in the dark.

"More, please," she panted, unable to form a sentence as his fingers did their slow dance. "The ache...I can't stand it."

He made an impatient sound and began rubbing in slow circles, heating her up, dipping his head to take her nipple into his mouth, then licking with forceful strokes. She slid toward an orgasm immediately, and when her muscles began to tremble, he brought his mouth to hers once more and kissed her deeply as she moaned her pleasure against his lips.

As she coasted down, she became aware of Killian's need. He was incredibly hard against her thigh and she slid her leg against him, looking into his dark, glittering eyes as he hovered above her.

"Are you going to make me beg you again?" she asked teasingly.

"Maybe," he said, jaw clenched as he fought to keep control.

He changed position slightly and she knew he was putting on a condom; after a few moments, she felt his massive hands around her waist and gasped in delight as he pulled her close. It quickly turned into a moan as he kissed her throat and turned his attention to her earlobe, nuzzling the soft spot just behind her jaw. She brought her hands down to find him, but he grabbed her wrists again and held them tightly above her head.

"Yes," she whispered. "Hold me down. Keep me safe."

It was too much. He slid up and into her with barely controlled force, a groan escaping him as he did so. He moved with long, slow strokes, pulling back as far as he could without leaving her before pushing forward again. She wrapped her legs around his waist and felt a giddy sort of pleasure bubbling up inside her chest. This was all she had ever wanted, to feel safe and loved by a man who also knew how to bring her to the brink of ecstasy.

Killian slowed his movements abruptly, and she knew he was trying to bring himself under control. She stilled, reveling in the feeling of him inside her.

"I think about you all day," he whispered against her ear.

"I think about you too," she said.

He let go of her wrists and she wrapped her arms around his neck, holding him close as he began moving within her again, building speed, and she matched his rhythm stroke for stroke. When she felt herself sliding toward orgasm, she clenched her muscles around him, immediately triggering his. He pulsed into her with a roar and grabbed the headboard with one hand to steady himself.

"Don't let me go," she panted, clinging to him. "Please don't let me go."

***

When Autumn's alarm went off at six-thirty, she still felt exhausted, but this time it was the good kind that came with sore muscles and sexual satisfaction. She'd slept off the tiredness and was ready to talk to Tana and Claire, to get some advice on what she needed to do for Brooke. With something of a game plan in mind, she showered and dressed, even choosing a new silk top that she'd bought with Killian in mind. It was a shimmery emerald green that made her pale skin glow, and she loved it.

Killian groaned and rolled over when she pulled the curtains open to let some sunlight stream into the room.

"What time is it?" he asked, shielding his eyes.

"A little after seven," she said, kneeling on the bed to kiss him. He pulled her down on top of him and she squealed laughter, bracing herself against his chest. "You be good, I can't be late. I need to talk to Tana."

"Damn, you look incredible. You sure you can't just stay in this bed with me all day?" he asked, dark eyes dancing with mischief.

"That's all I want to do, and I promise we'll do it soon, but I can't today," she said, giving him another quick kiss.

"Did you call someone about the windows?"

"Shit," she said, closing her eyes. "I totally forgot. Yesterday was so crazy."

"What about a security company?"

She squinted at him to try and make him laugh despite the stern look he was giving her; it worked.

"I'm sorry, I'm not the best adult," she said. "I'll take care of it today, I promise."

"Don't forget," he said.

"I won't," she said. "Oh, one more thing. There's a spare door key in the desk downstairs. Why don't you hang onto it so you can come and go whenever you want? I usually get home at the same time every night, but I don't want you to have to wait if I'm held up."

He stared at her for several moments, so long that she pulled back and sat on the bed.

"What's wrong?" she asked.

"You're giving me a key to your house?"

"Well yeah, I figured it makes sense. But if you're not comfortable with it—"

"No, no, it's fine. Better than fine. Thank you."

She studied his eyes. "Are you sure? I didn't mean to bypass a bunch of steps. I know this is new, but I want you to feel at home here."

"You don't…" he began and stopped. "I do feel at home."

He leaned forward and gave her the kind of kiss that turned her insides to mush. Her resolve weakened as he brushed his tongue against hers, and she pulled away with an effort shaking her finger at him.

"Only giving you something to remember me by today," he called as she grabbed her things and made a quick exit.

"No need for that," she whispered, touching her fingers to her lips with a smile.

***

Tana stared at her, mouth slack, eyes filled with the bright light of curiosity.

"Are you sure?" she asked.

"Positive," Autumn said. "Brooke isn't just using astral projection when she sleeps, she's figured out a way to manipulate that plane. It's how she found me at your parents' lake house. I was wide awake when she spoke to me. I thought for sure I was seeing her ghost, but it was her *soul*."

It had been a busy afternoon, and Autumn had put off talking to Tana about her experience until she knew they wouldn't be interrupted. Now the workday was nearly over, and darkness was swiftly falling outside the office window. Tana sat back in her chair, chewing thoughtfully on the tip of her pencil.

"So what can we do? Rose is never going to believe us."

"I was thinking about that," Autumn said. "If we can get in touch with Claire, if she could come to speak to Rose with us, it might help her see how serious we are."

Tana looked dubious. "I don't know. She's always struck me as the type of person who calls bullshit on a lot of things."

"I have to do something," I sighed. "Because the idea of Brooke leaving her body and wandering around in the world makes me want to scream with frustration. She's just so...small. Fragile. Seeing her in the woods last night—I wanted to cry, Tana."

"I know, babe," Tana said sympathetically. "Did you talk about any of this with Killian?"

Autumn shook her head. "We're not there yet. I only told you because you were there when Claire gave my reading."

"Would you really not have said anything otherwise?" Tana asked, shocked. "I'm your best friend."

"I know, but it sounds insane. It's almost too weird for me to believe, and I was there."

Tana searched her eyes. "It's a lot to take in, for sure, but I believe you. The question is, will Claire have any answers? Even if she agrees to talk to Rose, and even if Rose accepts what she tells her, there are no guarantees she'll be able to help Brooke. You need to be prepared for that, Autumn."

"I know. I am. But I have to try."

"Then I'll give her a call right now."

Tana picked up Claire's card and dialed the number just as David Mulligan walked into the office, looking grim.

"Hey, Chief," Autumn said, crossing her arms in front of her defensively. "I hope you've got some good news for me."

"I wish I did," he sighed, adjusting his gun belt. "None of your neighbors have cameras, not even those little doorbell ones, and no one saw anything that night. Did you check again to make sure nothing was taken? I hate to say it, but if they'd stolen something at least we could be looking for it at the pawnshops."

"They didn't take anything," Autumn said bitterly. "Which says to me that they just wanted to scare me and break my stuff. Who would take the time to do that other than two rich assholes who hate me for no good reason?"

"I know it seems like I'm not on your side, but I promise I am," David said quietly. "I've got my eye on them, but there's not a lot I can do right now. In the meantime, change your locks and get a security system."

"I'm on it," Autumn said. And then, because she felt bad, "I'm sorry for blowing up at you. It's not your fault. I'm just incredibly frustrated."

"I know you are," David said, and suddenly he looked older and incredibly weary. "I am, too. Some days, this job is easy as can be. Small towns usually have small crimes. But even when it's small, even when nobody gets hurt, it feels like I'm runnin' in circles trying to get things done for my people."

"What else is going on?" Autumn asked. "Still having trouble with that bear?"

"Yeah, but we're not sure it's a bear anymore. Some hunters from out of town had a run-in with it over the weekend. One dead, mauled pretty bad. His buddy got away without a scratch and told my deputy what he saw wasn't a bear at all. Said it looked like a big black dog."

"A dog?" Autumn repeated. "What kind of dog could do all that damage?"

"I don't know," David said, pushing up the brim of his hat to rub his forehead. "Got two men going door-to-door right now at all the houses around the woods, tellin' people to lock up their trash cans and bring in their pets, which is the protocol for a bear sighting. I don't know what else to do. Department don't have the money for search dogs, and we're at a dead end."

The click of a telephone receiver grabbed Autumn's attention and she turned to Tana, who looked up and shook her head.

"Claire isn't at the university today, and she's not answering her cell. I left a message with her assistant."

David's phone rang and he walked outside to answer as Autumn tried to formulate a game plan. She'd promised Brooke she would visit her, but she didn't want to go without backup from Claire. Knowing how sick Rose was only amplified the need for timeliness.

"Didn't Rose mention to you a while ago Brooke was having sleep issues?" Tana asked. "Maybe we could just suggest a doctor who can help or a sleep clinic. They might have some medication that would keep Brooke from traveling."

Autumn shook her head. "I'm not sure I want to go that route unless we have to. I can't explain why, but the idea of an outsider potentially finding out what Brooke is capable of scares me."

They sat in silence for a long moment, and when Tana spoke again, her voice was tense.

"You know, what you said was shitty."

Autumn turned to her in surprise. "What? What did I say?"

"That you wouldn't have told me about any of this if I hadn't been there for your reading with Claire. Do you know how that makes me feel? Like I've been best friends with a stranger for half my life."

Autumn flailed for the right words as she realized what she'd done, feeling the jagged pain of Tana's words hit her in the chest like knives. "Oh, Tana, I didn't mean it like th—"

"You meant it," Tana said. The hurt in her eyes outweighed the anger, and that was so much worse for Autumn to swallow. "Haven't I always had your back? Haven't I been there for you when no one else was?"

"Of course you have," Autumn said. Her voice trembled as she tried to retain control over her emotions and failed. "I'm so sorry, it was stupid of me. I tell you everything, you know that. You're my sister."

"You didn't tell me what the Napiers did to your house until the *next day*. That's fucked up, Autumn. You're different since you met Killian, you know. You even dress differently."

The words stung like scalding water on her skin. Autumn blinked back tears as David came back inside not wanting him to see her upset. He'd only ask questions, and she couldn't speak with any sense of normalcy.

"I hate to be the bearer of more bad news," he said heavily, placing his hands on his hips as he looked at the floor. "But Rose Napier died."

Tana sighed heavily and Autumn's eyes blurred with tears. She heard the creak of her chair as her friend leaned forward on the desk, and laid her head on her arms. More sounds assaulted her senses- traffic passing by on Main Street, the ticking of the clock on the wall above. The blood pumped in her veins as she pushed past David and out the door, running blindly down Main Street toward the trees that capped the dead end. She ran and ran, unmindful of the cold or the fact that she didn't have her coat. All she saw in her mind's eye was Rose's face superimposed over Brooke's and the pain that came with knowing she'd failed two people she cared about very much.

She might have walked for minutes or hours. Once full dark fell, there was no way of knowing. She wore no watch, guided only by the moonlight as she made her way through the woods of Pine Hollow. Some peripheral instinct told her the quarry was nearby on the right; perhaps it was the slightly metallic smell of the water below, or the curve of the trees as she walked deeper into the shadows. She pushed everything from her mind in an attempt to numb the pain, leaving herself a husk, and when she reached a clearing and looked up, she was startled to find the Napier mansion looming on the hill above her. She'd walked far, almost to the county line, and that scared her. It was like driving a long distance and suddenly realizing her mind had been on auto-pilot the entire time, and she had no memory of the journey.

Autumn slowed her walk as she approached the horse fence surrounding the property, looking at it up close for the first time in years. It seemed even more sinister under the moonlight— a formidable brick home with dozens of windows reflecting the night, like a spider's eyes. She wondered what was going on behind those walls and decided she didn't want to know. Tears prickled the back of her throat as she turned away, unwilling to think about all the questions swirling in her head.

She turned wearily to head back home, and ran headlong into someone, gasping in surprise as she backed up.

"Well, look who it is," Bill Napier said, chuckling softly. His nose was still bandaged from the fight with Killian. Above it, his eyes glittered in the moonlight. "We couldn't see the face on the surveillance cameras, just the person. Might be time to upgrade our *security system*, you think?"

Autumn's eyes narrowed. It was an obvious dig at her, a slap in the face after what they'd done to her home. Any other time, she might be fearful of meeting Bill Napier alone in the woods; now she only felt righteous anger.

"I was just leaving," she said.

"Now, now, hang on," Bill said, holding his hands up at chest level as if to stop her. "I just want to talk."

"I don't think we have much to say to each other," Autumn said. "Even if we did, we would probably be better off saying it in the daylight."

She turned away, ready to run if she needed to, but was stopped by Austin. He'd crept silently up behind her and stood with his thick arms folded across his chest, watching her with a smile. Did they not know about Rose yet? She didn't want to be the one to tell them, that was for damn sure.

"What is this?" she asked, turning back to Bill. "I told you, I was leaving. I didn't mean to come so close to your house. I was just out for a walk."

"Out for a walk in the dark, when there's a deadly beast on the loose?" Bill tutted. "Not a good idea for a little girl."

"Good thing I'm not a little girl, then," she said tightly.

Bill's eyes flicked toward Austin; she saw it a second too late. Before she could run, Austin's vise-like arms wrapped around her, trapping her in place. She struggled, kicking her feet to try and make contact against his shins, but he laughed at her efforts.

"You shouldn't have come here," Bill said softly, moving toward her. He reached up and slid a finger down her cheek and she recoiled, turning her face away. "Bad things happen to people alone in the woods."

His hand dropped to the collar of her silk blouse, gently slipping across the buttons before suddenly yanking roughly, ripping the fabric clean down the middle. She gasped as the cold night air hit her bare skin and stood shivering in her bra, straining against Austin's grip. Her skin bruised beneath his arms and she steeled herself to fight, eyeing Bill warily as he backed up a step and stared at her.

When a dark blur flew by, Autumn thought at first it was a shadow of some sort, but then there was the roar of an animal, and Austin's arms loosened their grip. Seeing her chance, she brought her heel down as hard as she could on the top of his foot and he howled, releasing her as he stumbled backward.

"Bill," he called—and that was when the screams began.

Autumn turned to find Bill but didn't understand what she was seeing. A cloud had passed over the moon, leaving them in the sort of final darkness that came with diving too deep into the ocean. From where she stood, it looked like a huge black shadow had battened onto Bill's body, a shadow that slowly revealed itself to be a massive, angry beast. Bill whirled around, trying to throw it off, but it clung stubbornly to him. As her eyes adjusted to the lack of light, she saw the sleeve of his coat had been ripped away, and the dark bloom of blood on the shirt beneath.

The bear, she thought wildly, *or maybe a wolf.* The thing the Chief had warned them about.

"Help me," Bill cried, stumbling across the rocky hillside as the animal roared thunderously. It held onto him but stretched on its hind legs, towering over him.

"I'm going to get a gun," Austin screamed, and then he was gone, leaving his brother and Autumn alone with the beast.

Bill swung his arms wildly and managed to land a punch. The animal was flung off him and landed with a grunt on the leaf-strewn ground. Bill lunged away, running awkwardly up the hill toward the house without looking back.

Autumn began slowly backing away, trying to calculate the odds she could outrun the creature once it caught its breath. It was panting heavily, already moving slowly in the leaves to get up. As the clouds moved on to reveal the full moon, the massive animal—a wolf—shifted and morphed as it stood up. The fur slowly disappeared from its body, and Autumn saw the barrel-chested shape of a familiar man appear in its place.

"Autumn?" Killian said, taking cautious steps toward her. He was naked, bloody, his breath pluming in the air before him. The sweat on his body steamed slightly. "Don't be scared."

She didn't realize she was moving backward until she tripped over a branch and fell, shooting out her hands to catch herself. She scooted away from him on her butt, her hair in her eyes, sharp pine needles and twigs scratching at her palms, but not caring.

She realized, too late, what had been nagging her. The realization that the dream she'd had of Killian covered in blood hadn't been a dream at all, but a journey through astral projection.

Chapter Nine

"Autumn, it's me," Killian said, advancing slowly toward her. "I'm not going to hurt you."

She stopped short and scrambled to her feet, keeping her eyes locked on him. It was Killian, alright, naked as the day he was born and covered in blood. She realized she was panting both from fear and the effort to retain body heat and forced herself to calm down, take deep breaths.

"What...the fuck," she managed. "What are you?"

He was panting as well. He inhaled and forcibly relaxed his shoulders, closed his eyes briefly. "I don't think it's going to be any more believable if I say it out loud."

Her entire body began to shake violently, and she steadied herself against a tree. Killian walked closer with arms outstretched, ready to help, but stopped when she looked up at him.

"What are you doing out here?" she asked in a shaking voice. "My God, have you been attacking people? Chief said a man was killed over the weekend, a hunter..."

"That wasn't me," Killian said. "Listen, Austin said he was going for a gun and I believe him. We need to get out of here."

She watched him walk further into the trees and retrieve a dark bundle: his clothes. He yanked on his jeans, t-shirt, and boots and returned to her with a look of furious determination on his face.

"Are you hurt?" she asked breathlessly, eyeing the blood on his arms.

"It's not mine," he said. "Come on. I'm going to carry you out of here before you freeze to death."

He picked her up before she could protest, cradling her against his chest. She was too cold and too tired to fight it, curling up into his warmth as he ran through the trees.

Minutes passed; she might have nodded off in his arms but wasn't sure. *Shock*, she thought, *I'm going into shock*. Above them, the sky had cleared into a bright, starry blue. She watched the tops of the trees as Killian ran, putting together puzzle pieces in her mind. His warmth, his strength, his refusal to tell her why he was in Pine Hollow. His absences. And, of course, her dream, which had shown him covered in blood. Had she stumbled upon him while he was hunting? Unknowingly cast her mind out to him and projected herself into the real world as he ran through the trees after his prey?

"Autumn?" he said softly.

She looked up at him, blinking sleepily as she tried to focus.

"We're home. I'm going to get you warm and call the Chief."

She wanted to say so many things, to tell him she was okay and not to bother, but she could only nod. In a few moments, she was safely on her couch wrapped in warm blankets.

Killian brought her a steaming mug of tea. She cradled it in both hands and sipped occasionally, and after several minutes she began to feel more or less like herself again. Killian was pacing back and forth across the living room floor. He clenched and unclenched his fists, his face grim.

When someone knocked on the door, Autumn jumped. Killian let David in and stood by the door as if to guard it.

"Autumn? What happened?" David asked softly, kneeling in front of her.

I was about to be raped by two thugs then a wolf jumped out of the shadows, oh, and did I mention it turned into a man, my current lover?

She swallowed and waited a moment, looking for her voice. The last thing she wanted to do was break down into hysterical tears in front of him, or find herself in a police car headed for an asylum.

"I was...attacked," she said haltingly. "In the woods."

"Me and Tana went out after you, but by the time we got to the street you were already gone," he said apologetically. "Why did you go into the woods?"

"I don't know. I was upset because of Rose and I ran," she said. "I didn't realize how far I'd gone until I looked up and saw the Napiers' mansion. I didn't mean to go that far."

"Who attacked you?" he asked, maintaining gentle eye contact. "Do you need me to get you to the hospital?"

She shook her head violently. She didn't want the entire town to know what had happened, and a trip to the hospital—where most of the staff knew her from work—would ensure lots of gossip.

"I was getting ready to leave and go back to the office when Bill and Austin showed up," she said hoarsely. A lump had formed in her throat. Getting her story out would prove harder than she'd thought. "They saw me on the security cameras, they said. I told them I was going to leave but Austin grabbed me and held me. He w-wouldn't let me go."

David took a deep breath. He looked upset. "Then what happened?"

"Then..." she faltered, embarrassment creeping up and coloring her cheeks. David was watching her expectantly. She had to tell the whole truth. "Then Bill ripped my shirt open."

Killian sucked in a sharp breath over by the door. She could practically feel him grinding his teeth. For the first time, she wondered whether this might be the thing that would push him over the edge with Bill. Now that she knew what he was, she had no trouble imagining him being capable of murder.

"But then an animal came out of the trees and attacked him," she said quickly, "And it was huge. It must have been the one you're looking for. It jumped on Bill and hurt him pretty bad. I stomped Austin's foot and he let go of me, and he ran away. To get a gun, he said. Bill fought the thing off and ran back up to the house."

"The animal must have been hurt and crawled back into the woods," Killian said. "I was worried about Autumn because she was late coming home, so I went by the office. Tana told me what happened so I went out looking for her. Good thing I found her when I did, she was freezing and going into shock."

David stood up and measured Killian with his gaze. "And who are you, son?"

"Killian Quint, sir. I'm visiting from Seattle."

He held his hand out to shake and Autumn realized he'd cleaned the blood off his arm sometime in the minutes between their return home and David's arrival.

"Good man, Quint," David said. "You were a hero tonight."

"Yeah, well, I hope you're ready to arrest those assholes because I'm not going to rest until you do," Killian said, crossing his powerful arms.

David turned solemnly to Autumn. "If you're ready to press assault charges, I'll need to take an official statement. That means I have to take pictures of you."

Autumn took a deep breath and nodded. "It's okay."

She retold her story so Chief could transcribe it, and he gave her a copy to keep. She could see Killian in her peripheral but purposely kept her gaze on the floor to avoid looking him in the eye, afraid of what she might see there. Who was this man she'd come to love? He had transformed from a beast right in front of her, turning back into the protective and caring person she thought she knew. In her mind and heart and all the spaces in between, she felt confused.

"Okay, darlin', this is the hard part," David said gently, pulling out his phone. "I need you to stand up and take the blankets off."

Again, Autumn kept her eyes down as she stood and let the blankets fall to the ripped-up couch, so she heard rather than saw the shock and dismay the two men felt at the sight of her. She waited for the camera to click twice, heard David ask her to turn around, saw the flash go off two more times. When he instructed her to turn again and remove the rest of her shirt, she slid it easily from her shoulders and let the tattered silk fall to the floor. Fresh tears fell from her eyes as she remembered how much care she'd taken to dress that morning, choosing the top because she knew Killian would like it.

"Jesus Christ," Killian said, his jaw clenched so tightly she was afraid he might break his teeth. "Jesus fucking Christ."

Her ribs were tender; she realized it hurt to take deep breaths and resolved to take shallow ones. Looking down, she saw great purple bruises extending from the band of her bra to her waist, as well as around the middle of her upper arms: gifts from Austin.

David snapped several more pictures, looking pained as he did so, and then picked up one of the blankets to cover her again.

"I'm so sorry this happened to you," he said softly. "They will be punished."

He left with a sharp look at Killian that Autumn couldn't read. While Killian paced the room, Autumn waited until David's car was halfway down the street, tail lights flashing in the dark, before she stood up.

"I'm going to shower," she murmured dully. Killian was silent. Autumn went into the bathroom and shed the rest of her ruined clothes. The back of her pants was mud-stained and bloody, remainders from Killian's arms as he'd carried her through the woods.

***

The hot shower felt heavenly.

Autumn stood under the spray for several minutes and let it scald her skin, knowing it was the only way she would be able to sleep later. She wouldn't feel clean otherwise.

Am I dreaming all this? Am I in another world, a dream state? How else could a wolf turn into a man?

She asked the questions, but Autumn already knew the answers.

When she was finished, tucked safely into her warm bathrobe, she walked into the bedroom to find Killian waiting for her. He sat on the edge of the bed, hands folded, head down. She remembered the feel of his arms beneath her as they walked through the trees, how he'd attacked Bill in the shape of a wolf to save her. If Bill or Austin had carried a weapon, she realized, Kilian could have been seriously hurt or killed. At the very least, he would probably have revealed his human form as a result. But he'd given no thought to his safety. Only hers.

She stepped slowly toward him and put a gentle hand on his head, running her fingers through his hair. He made no move to look up but leaned forward slightly so that his forehead was resting on her belly.

"I don't care what you are," she said softly. "I'm sorry I reacted the way I did in the woods."

He looked up then, his dark eyes so full of emotion she was startled. She felt her own eyes widen as tears spilled down his cheeks and he wrapped his arms around her hips to hold her close.

"I thought I was going to lose you," he said thickly. "I never want to feel that way again."

"You're not going to lose me," she said, her throat choked with tears. She let him pull her down into his lap, to cradle her.

"I'm sorry about Rose Napier," he said, stroking her hair. "I wish I could have been with you when you got the news. None of this would have happened."

"It happened because I was so focused on myself I blocked out the rest of the world," she said. "It was all my fault."

"No," he said firmly, placing his hands on either side of her face and holding her gaze. "The blame doesn't lay on you. Don't say that."

She closed her eyes, holding back the tears, and lay against his chest.

When the doorbell rang several moments later, Killian jerked his head up and stood suddenly, depositing her safely on the bed.

"Stay here," he commanded. "And yes, I know we need to talk still about what you saw. About what I am."

Then he was gone, and Autumn's heart sped up in her chest as she listened to his footsteps on the stairs. After a beat, the door opened and Tana's worried voice drifted up. Autumn ran out to the landing, a sob escaping her as she saw her closest friend in the world standing in the open doorway with tears on her face.

"I'm so sorry," she said as she stumbled down the stairs. "Please forgive me."

Tana held her arms out and clutched Autumn to her tightly, her voice shaking. "Nothing to forgive, baby. I'm the one who's sorry."

Killian closed the door behind them and the two friends moved to the couch, where they sat in an embrace for a long time. Tana rubbed Autumn's back in slow circles as she cried silently, knowing she would dream about this night over and over in the coming weeks.

"David called and told me to get over here quick, but he didn't tell me the whole story," Tana said after a while. "You feel like talkin' about it?"

Slowly, with encouragement from Killian as he sat beside her on the couch, Autumn relayed the story of her run-in with the Napiers. She sensed Tana's anger mounting with every word, knowing she felt as frustrated as Autumn did. Even if David arrested both brothers, they'd only make bail and ensure the judge was in their pocket.

When Autumn finished, Tana turned to Killian with shimmery eyes.

"Good thing you were there," she said. "But how did you find her?"

"She was late getting home, and when she didn't answer her phone I got worried, so I went out looking for her in the woods. I thought she might have taken a walk."

Autumn frowned. She was tired and still recovering from the shock, but she was sure he'd said the same thing to David earlier, only switched around. That he'd spoken to Tana, who'd pointed him to the woods. She looked questioningly at him but he kept his gaze on Tana, not meeting her eyes.

"That's a lot of ground to cover if she made it to the Napiers," Tana said. "She's lucky you're so fast. Thank god you were there."

She hugged Autumn close, then pulled away to look at her.

"Stay home tomorrow. Keep your phone with you at all times, I'll be calling to check on you."

Autumn was already shaking her head. "I can't leave you alone at the office, there's so much to do now that Rose…" she faltered, unable to get the words out.

"I mean it," Tana said. "You need the rest. Rose would agree with me. Besides, you're not gonna be any good to Brooke if you're not taking care of yourself."

"Where is she? Have you spoken to her?"

"Right now she's at her house with a state-appointed guardian," Tana sighed. "She'll stay there tonight and they'll take her to a facility in the morning, where she'll remain until the court settles her case. David said he'll let us know what the arrangements are for Rose as soon as he hears something."

"Brooke must be so scared," Autumn said. "I wish I could go see her."

"Don't worry about that right now," Tana said. "Brooke is a strong kid and she knows you're here for her. We're going to help her through this. And I'll keep calling Claire about that other thing, okay?"

Autumn nodded and they embraced once more. Knowing Brooke was with a stranger, scared and sad after the loss of her mother, made Autumn want to scream, but she knew there was nothing to be done at the moment. Brooke's fate lay in the hands of a judge.

After Tana left, Autumn sat back down on the couch and let the silence of the house fall over her. The events of the day had left her feeling hollowed out and all she wanted to do was sleep, but it was only eight o'clock. When Killian moved closer and took her hand, she looked up at him.

"Tell me," she said softly. "The truth about why you were in the woods. About why you're here."

He ran a hand through his hair, leaving it standing in short spikes. "I'm sorry I had to lie about that to David and Tana. There was no other way."

She nodded. "I figured as much."

"You know I'm here in Pine Hollow to look for someone," he began. "I don't have a name, I have no idea if it's a man or a woman, and I don't have an address. All I know...what I think I know...is that they're extremely powerful and that they've built a drug empire here."

Autumn smiled, confused. "What? In Pine Hollow? That's not possible."

"Do you remember me telling you about my friends Amy and Brian?" he asked.

"The ones who drove through here and told you how great it was?"

He nodded. "Amy is...like me."

"A werewolf." *Finally,* she got to say the word, the word she'd been mulling over since the incident in the woods. She'd thought saying it aloud would make her feel silly, that Killian would laugh at her and offer some other explanation. Instead, he looked as grave as she'd ever seen him.

"Yes. When they came through here, they stopped at the quarry to eat lunch and she smelled others like us nearby. Werewolves have a powerful scent. It can carry for miles, especially when we're sick. What she smelled was a deep illness that had been going on for a long time."

"Sick how?"

"In this case, it was from being kept in wolf form against their will," he said. "Brian doesn't know about Amy yet, so she couldn't stay here and try to track the scent herself. I told her I would come and take over. We have reason to believe someone has captured men and women like me and is purposely preventing them from cycling somehow, keeping them in wolf form."

Autumn considered that for a moment, thinking about all the things she'd seen and read about werewolves. "But I thought the moon...doesn't it control those phases?"

"It does, but it's complicated," he said, looking pained. "The moon is a catalyst for change. The process can be interrupted, prolonged, or stopped altogether with the use of certain drugs or plants. If that happens long enough, the person affected grows extremely sick, both physically and mentally. They start to feel extreme pain all over, and the only thing that helps in any measure is to kill, to drink blood."

Autumn felt her eyes widen. "The deer, the hunter."

Killian nodded. "We believe this person is keeping werewolves captive so they can use them for something. Based on Amy's experience here and what I've found myself, I think they're making these wolves guard a drug den. It worries me that there's been a murder. Once there's a taste of human blood, nothing else ever satisfies."

"This is crazy," Autumn said. "I know there are dark places in Pine Hollow, but to think there's a major drug kingpin hiding here, doing terrible things to these people...it's hard to wrap my head around."

Listen to me. Drug kingpin? What about the damned werewolves? I'm more at ease with the latter than the former.

"The problem is I'm running out of time. Whenever I feel like I'm getting close to what I'm looking for, things change. The wind carries scents pretty far, and it's worse around the quarry."

"What happens when time runs out? And how much of it do you have?"

"Three days," he said roughly. "The moon phases and the seasons affect us powerfully. When the fall equinox comes, if those wolves are still unable to phase, they'll get stuck in that form forever."

Autumn let that sink in for a moment, her mind so full of swirling thoughts that she felt dizzy.

"Oh my god," she said suddenly. "You were in the woods tonight because you think...because you believe that..."

He nodded. "The Napiers are the ones I'm looking for."

***

Later, while Killian was in the shower, Autumn lay in bed consumed by her thoughts.

The grief and worry she felt in regards to Rose and Brooke held one part of her mind; Killian, the other. She had no room for the

Napiers, either mentally or emotionally, so she focused on the man she had come to love in a matter of days.

But he wasn't a man. He was *other*. A beast, a changeling, a cursed being. He hadn't offered any truths about how it had come to be and she hadn't asked, afraid of the answers. She thought of all the horror movies she'd seen, all the books she'd read that dealt with the occult and wondered why she didn't feel more afraid. Even after seeing what he was—the transformation beneath a cold moon—she couldn't bring herself to fear him or the things he might be capable of. Maybe, she thought, because she'd already seen so many terrible things from the humans in her life.

Remembering what he'd said about the poor creatures who were being held captive, she shuddered. What if Killian was captured? Forced to stay in wolf form against his will, made to endure the pain the human body could never withstand? Even as strong as he was, she couldn't imagine him lasting long under those conditions. The thought twisted her insides into knots.

When he emerged from the bathroom in a cloud of steam, she sat up in bed and stretched out her arms toward him. He hesitated, and she realized he was fully dressed.

"What's wrong?" she asked, dropping her arms.

"I was just thinking—maybe I should go."

The sinking feeling in her stomach at the thought of Killian in pain began to swell, crowding her organs and making it hard to breathe.

"What? Why?"

"You've seen what I am," he said simply. "You know the damage I can do. You're part of this now. I didn't want you to be involved in any way, but I failed. I fucked it all up, Autumn. You're in danger now because of me. If the Napiers are the people I'm looking for, they'll be hunting me. They have my scent on Bill's clothes, they can send one of their wolves to find me."

"You didn't fail at anything," she said, her voice shivering with the effort of holding back tears. "You saved me from two men who were going to cause me harm. Twice. I told you, I don't care what you are..."

"Yes, and that is insanely kind and loving, so much so that it blows my fucking mind, honestly," Killian said. "But it's also very naive. You *should* care. This morning when you suggested the house key, I felt like crying because I knew that no matter how much sweetness you offered me, I couldn't keep accepting it. And I've had so little of it lately."

"But why can't you accept it?" she asked, holding out her hand for him to take. He did, reluctantly, and sat on the edge of the bed. "I'm not afraid of you. I'm not afraid of the Napiers. Maybe that's naive, or maybe it's because I've seen so much misery and violence it doesn't affect me anymore. My grandma once said I had a darkness that lived in me, that I carry it around. I guess she was right."

Killian shook his head and lightly touched her chest, right above her heart. "There's no darkness here. I told you, you shine. I saw it the first time we met, on that curvy little road in the woods. You've got a light that no one else has."

She smiled up at him, a genuine smile that felt good on her face. "So stay."

He smiled, too, only briefly. It faded after a moment and was replaced with a look of concern.

"I hate myself for not being strong enough to leave," he said.

His hand was still in hers; she pulled him toward her and lay back until he was hovering over her in the bed. With both hands, she touched his face, rubbed the back of his neck, slid her palms down the hard muscles of his chest. His brow was furrowed into a frown, his expression angry, and she stilled her hands abruptly.

"Please don't be upset with me," she whispered. "I know I'm being selfish. I just can't bear the thought of you leaving, Killian."

"You think I'm upset with you?" he asked, his voice hoarse with emotion. "That's not what this is. I'm afraid I'm going to hurt you."

"You won't," she said, pulling him closer.

He kept his weight on his hands, refusing to touch her with his body. "You're breakable. I'm a goddamn wrecking ball."

"I'm bruised up," she said. "Not broken. And you have no idea how much I want to feel the weight of you on me right now. Please."

Slowly, he relented, moving lower until he could support himself on his forearms on either side of her. She kissed him and he kissed back, tenderly, gliding his fingertips along the edge of her jaw.

"Where did they hurt you?" he asked roughly.

"Only my arms and ribs," she said, keeping her hands on his face to keep him calm.

118

"Did Bill...did he touch you?" he asked, his voice as taut as piano wire.

"No," she said quickly.

He studied her eyes for a moment. "You will never know what it took for me not to kill him."

"Don't think about that now," she said with a shiver. "Just touch me."

With infinite care, he slid one hand down her side and rested it on her hip, caressing the silky skin there for a moment before moving on to the top of her thigh. She sighed as his fingers explored the soft folds of her, and was overcome by the urge to fill her hands with him. This time he didn't pull away or pin her hands to the bed. Beneath his shorts he was unyielding and in her palms, he was hot and throbbing, allowing her to stroke and tease as much as she wanted.

And when they were both stripped of clothing, he held her like a fragile piece of crystal as he moved within her, strong arms keeping her safely caged.

Chapter Ten

When morning came, Autumn could barely move.

She opened her eyes with effort and tried to roll toward Killian but was met with exquisite pain that rampaged through her entire body. She felt like she'd been hit by a bus.

"What's wrong?" Killian asked in alarm, and she realized she'd cried out.

"I'm hurting," she managed and lay still on her back to try and calm her sore muscles and ribs. *Austin must have superhuman strength*, she thought bitterly, remembering the feel of his vise-like arms around her.

Killian went to the bathroom and returned with a large glass of water and four tiny pills, which she recognized as a pain reliever. She swallowed them down and lay back, focusing on relaxing each group of muscles one at a time. After a few minutes, she felt a little better and checked the clock on her nightstand, astonished to see that it was nearly eleven a.m.

"What can I do for you?" he asked, watching her in concern.

"Nothing. It's only a little stiffness. I must have slept curled up last night."

He nodded. "You sounded like you were having some pretty bad dreams."

"I'm sorry," she said with a grimace. "I hope I didn't keep you awake."

"I stayed up through the night to watch over you and the house," he said, sitting beside her on the bed. "I kept wanting to wake you up, but every time I thought about it you'd settle down again."

"You didn't have to do that. You must be exhausted."

"Nah. We werewolves can go a long time without sleep."

The word startled her and she struggled to sit up in bed so she could look him in the eyes. The previous day had been so fraught with drama and stress that her mind had barely been able to settle on one thing to worry about. Now it all came crashing into her like a speeding train.

"Are you okay?" she asked. "Bill didn't hurt you, did he?"

"He was strong, but he wasn't a match for me in wolf form," Killian said. "He hit me and I let go of him so I could make sure you were alright. I'm fine. "

He was distracted, moody. She touched his brow lightly, wishing she could take the weight of his thoughts into her head.

"Will you tell me what your plan is? I'd like to help," she said.

It was the wrong thing to say. His already tense mood darkened even further seemingly at the idea of involving her.

"No, you won't help," he said. "You're going to stay here tonight while I check out the grounds of the Napier house. David stopped by earlier and said he'd taken them both into custody. Bill had to go to the emergency room last night to get stitches in his arm and he told the nurse he'd been attacked by a wild animal in the woods, which corroborates your story."

"They won't be in jail long," she said. "They've probably already made bail."

"David said Judge Hoskins is out of town, some kind of family emergency. He won't be back until tomorrow, which means they'll be sitting in that cell at least for tonight, and maybe tomorrow night too."

"So your plan is to wait until dark and go investigate their house?" Autumn asked. "They have tons of security. Plus, Bill and Austin aren't the only ones who live there."

"Yeah, I did some research on old man Napier," Killian said. "He hasn't been in the best of health in the last couple of years, which is why his boys stay there. I'm betting they're helping out with a lot more than housework."

"You think he's running a drug operation and they're...what? His lackeys?"

"I think Michael is strictly behind-the-scenes, a puppet master. Bill and Austin are the ones with connections, but they aren't the only ones who know people. That's why I had to do some traveling over the weekend. I've got solid info on the narcotics running out of this place and they branch out into every direction. If I'm right about the Napiers, this is way bigger than just Pine Hollow. They've reached into Tennessee, Ohio, Indiana, maybe as far south as

Florida, and I'm betting they're adding onto their werewolf army every day, taking new ones in different cities."

Autumn pondered that for a moment. "I don't like this at all. Don't get me wrong, you're the strongest person I know, but you'll be walking into unfamiliar territory with no backup and no weapons. You have no idea what they're capable of. And how are you even going to get past their cameras?"

"It's overcast," he said, looking thoughtfully out the window. "The moon will be hidden tonight. In my other form, I'll be a shadow among shadows. Besides, I don't have a choice. Tomorrow is the equinox."

He made no effort to argue her point about how vulnerable he would be, and that scared her more than anything. He was determined to push through and finish what he'd started, and nothing she said would make any difference.

It might be for the best, a voice whispered in her mind. These men were Brooke's last surviving family members. If Killian could find evidence of illegal activity that would put them away forever, Brooke would be spared their guardianship. She would have a chance at something better.

Autumn raked her hair back from her forehead. A massive stress headache had begun thumping there like a bass drum. She wished she could go back to sleep and forget about the world for a while.

"I don't understand why they're doing all this...holding people captive, building their little army of guards...just for some pot fields," she said.

Killian turned to her, his dark eyes serious.

"I don't think it's pot they're protecting," he said. "They've got fifty acres out there. Plenty of room for poppy fields."

Autumn's eyes widened. "Heroin? I don't know. There have been rumors that the Napiers were involved in some shady stuff for years, and David has kept an eye on them because of it. Wouldn't a heroin business be kind of hard to hide?"

"In a bigger town, maybe. But I don't think the Pine Hollow Police Department has the resources to handle something like this. Even if David had probable cause to search the property—and he wouldn't, because the Napiers are too smart to let that happen—he'd have to comb every inch of those fifty acres by hand to find what he's looking for. I think the poppies are well hidden."

Autumn thought about what David had said the day before, wishing he had access to dogs that could help him sniff out the wild animal in the woods.

"Yeah, I think you're right," she said. "Which reminds me, I want you to be extra careful when you change form. David has his men patrolling the woods when they can spare the time, and they won't hesitate to shoot if they see you."

"I know," he said, smiling at her concern. "This has been my life for a long time and I'm experienced in looking after myself, I promise. I can hear people coming from a mile away."

She took his hand in hers, tracing the lines on his palm with a finger. His skin was rough, calloused, and she couldn't imagine how he managed to touch her so softly. But he always did, and he'd bared his soul to her so much in the past eighteen hours she couldn't keep quiet about *her* secret anymore. It bubbled up inside her throat, threatening to scald her if she didn't release it.

"I need to tell you something," she said. "It's hard to understand, and it may change the way you feel about me. I'm sorry I didn't tell you about it before."

He squeezed her hand gently. "There's nothing you can say that will change the way I feel about you."

She hesitated, unsure of where to begin, and then cleared her throat. "Since I was a little girl, I've had vivid dreams. Nightmares, a lot of them. Sometimes I get active or even violent in my sleep...I guess you got a taste of that last night...and sometimes...sometimes, something else happens."

"Do you sleepwalk?"

"No. At least, I don't think so," she said and took a deep breath. "I'm a traveler."

He studied her eyes. "What do you mean?"

"When I sleep, if I focus hard on something, I can force myself out of my body. It's called astral projection, but I never realized that's what I was doing until recently. My soul can go in whatever direction I want it to, but my body stays in bed."

Killian frowned, turning his body toward hers. "Isn't that dangerous?"

"Yes. There's the possibility that something could happen to me while I'm traveling...I could get lost or stuck somewhere...or, if you believe in such things, a demon could come along and take possession of my body while my soul is elsewhere."

"How do you know all this?"

"A friend of Tana's family read my palm over the weekend," she explained. "She's an expert in the field, a professor, in fact. She saw it all in my hand. If she'd told me the same thing five years ago, I might not have believed her, but after the experiences I've had lately, I'm inclined to take her at her word."

He was silent for several moments, looking at their interlocked fingers. When he spoke again, the concern in his voice was thick.

"Is there a way for you to control it?"

"There are some things I can do," she said. "It's not easy, though."

"So last night, were you…?

"No," she said quickly. "That's what makes it so tricky to deal with. I can't always tell the difference between a nightmare or a vivid dream and the kind where I'm traveling. I've been doing this since I was young, so unlearning it is going to take some time."

"Was there something that caused these nightmares when you were younger?" he asked cautiously.

She nodded. "Lots of things. Trauma, abuse, stress. My father was...not a good man. He used his fists a lot, he was verbally abusive, he used to play little mind games to make me and my mom feel like we were the crazy ones. And that was just when he was home, which wasn't often."

Killian's jaw tightened. "You said home was a toxic environment. I didn't realize how bad it was."

"Pretty bad," she said. "There's a lot that I've blocked out. Sometimes a memory will pop up in a dream and it completely ruins my day. Claire told me that one of my recurring dreams is a memory of being kidnapped, but I have no recollection of it happening. My parents never talked about it afterward. I don't know how I got home."

"Jesus," Killian said. He squeezed her hand, gently.

"The worst thing was losing my mother," she said, picking at a loose thread on the comforter. "I used to dream about her all the time, but those dreams stopped. I'm starting to worry I'll forget what she looked like. When I left home, I didn't take much. Just my clothes and my toothbrush, and I left everything else with my dad. I don't even have any photos of her."

Killian picked up her hand and kissed it. "You are the bravest person I know. I can't imagine doing that at sixteen, especially after going through everything you endured."

Autumn shrugged. "I've never felt very brave. More like the exact opposite, scared of everything."

"That's what bravery is all about. Being scared to do something and doing it anyway. Look at everything you do at work, all the battles you've fought for your clients. You're a badass, Autumn."

"If you say so," she said with a laugh. "Listen...I have a question, and you don't have to answer if you don't want to."

"How did I become a werewolf?" he asked. The corners of his mouth turned up slightly as he looked at her.

Autumn nodded. "Is it something someone did to you? Or were you born..."

"Nah, my family is as normal as they come. Everything I told you on our first date was true, you know. I've had to keep some things from you and I'm not proud of that, but I tried to tell the entire truth about everything else."

"I know," she said. "I understand why you did it."

"I was attacked as a kid," he said. "In the woods where I was camping with some friends. It was the summer I turned thirteen, and I got up in the middle of the night to use the bathroom. I didn't hear anything until the wolf was on me."

"My god," Autumn whispered. "You must have been so scared."

"The fear came afterward when I realized how bad I was hurt," he said, his eyes taking on a faraway look as he remembered. "And in the days after that, when I realized what I was becoming. It was...painful."

"Do you know who it was?"

"I never came across them again. I didn't meet another werewolf until I was an adult."

"How many do you think there are? In the United States, I mean."

"Hard to say. Probably a lot more than you might think." He was silent for a moment. "You said you've been having experiences. What happened?"

She nodded. "While I was at the lake house with Tana, Brooke showed up. In spirit form. She's a traveler, too."

"Seriously? What are the odds?" Killian asked in surprise.

"I don't know. What scares me is that Brooke made herself visible to me somehow. She can manipulate the real world while she's dreaming, she can touch things and they can touch her. When I travel, the things around me feel insubstantial. It's almost like walking around as a ghost. No one can see or hear me. But for her...she's very powerful, Killian."

"My god," Killian said, and she could see that the possibilities and ramifications of what she'd just said were streaming through his mind. "No wonder you've been so worried about her."

"It's a big part of the reason," she agreed. "Her relationship with her uncles is another."

She leaned her head on his shoulder and he kissed her crown, his hand never leaving hers. After a few moments, she'd gathered enough strength to mention the thing that had been nagging her for days.

"Killian, I had a dream about you on the night of our first date. Well, I thought it was a dream. Now I think I was projecting and didn't realize it."

"Really?" he asked, curious. "What happened?"

"I followed you as you ran through the woods. You were bare-chested and covered in blood, howling up at the sky."

His hand jerked in hers as he met her eyes, startled. "What?"

Autumn took a deep breath, thinking of Claire's words to her at the lake house. *I think he has inherent goodness in him. But he's also constantly changing. Not volatile, but....shifting. Adapting. Not a danger to you, but perhaps a liability in some way that might not make sense to you now.*

"I told you before that I don't care what you are, and I meant that," she said. "It doesn't change my feelings a bit. But I need to know whose blood that was."

He rested the back of his head on the wall and sighed. "I can't imagine how that must have looked to you. That part of my life is so ugly."

"Not ugly," she said. "Maybe a little worrisome."

He laughed and shook his head. "Only you would say that. I promise it looked worse than it was. I have a measure of control.

When I get the urge to change, I hunt. It's instinctual. I can't completely fight it, but I can alter it. Small animals only, rabbits and things like that."

"You can alter it?" she asked. "Does that mean you're fully aware of everything when you're in wolf form?"

"Yes. Not always, not in the beginning. Over the years I've learned how to merge both sides of my consciousness so I can stay in control."

"Sounds like you could teach me some things," Autumn said with a little smile.

"Only if you aren't scared of me," he said, his voice deepening. "Are you scared?"

"Of course not," she said.

"You know, I meant it when I said it would be better if you were. But I can't help but be relieved you're not running away screaming at the sight of me."

"That's not going to happen," she said. "You've said before you were worried about hurting me. Is it because you're afraid you'll lose control and change?"

"That's a big part of it," he said softly. "The older I get, the easier it is to keep control over the transformation. But navigating new situations is always tricky, and I've never met anyone like you. There's no precedent for these feelings."

She pulled herself up and over him, straddling his lap so she could face him. His eyes were half-lidded with desire, his strong hands gripping her waist. He kissed her softly, sliding his hands beneath her t-shirt to tickle her back, and she shivered.

"Tell me how I can keep you safe if you're traveling in your sleep," he said against her mouth.

"I guess you'll have to keep me awake," she said, rubbing herself gently against his jean-clad lap. He was already hard, pressing against her underwear; she held his gaze closely to see the pleasure blooming in his eyes.

He pulled her t-shirt up and off, capturing a taut nipple in his mouth. She dipped her head and kissed his neck, moving up to pay attention to his earlobe and the soft spot behind his jaw. When he moaned and clutched her tighter, she pulled away and arched her back in the tangerine light streaming in through the windows. With a deep growl low in his throat, he wrapped his arms around her waist and brought her closer, crushing her to him as he brought his mouth to her neck, her chest, her breasts, anywhere he could reach.

She reached down and unzipped his pants, releasing him with care. With one hand wrapped around him, she moved her panties aside and slid herself against the sensitive head of his cock, teasing him to the brink. He grabbed her ass in both hands, struggling to keep control, but she just smiled and slid up, out of his reach.

"Not so fast," she said softly. "This is going to take a while."

***

They spent the afternoon in bed, worshipping one another.

After her battle with the Napiers and the news about Rose, after weeks of worrying about Brooke's fate and months of not sleeping well, Autumn needed a moment of selfishness. She didn't want to admit to herself she was pinning all her hopes on Killian's plan. That he would somehow discover the answer to so many of her problems once he made his way to that big mansion on the hill after nightfall—but in a way, she was. Forcing all other thoughts from her mind, she focused only on the smell and taste and feel of him and reveled in the way he looked at her, like she was a cool spring in the middle of the desert and he was a man dying of thirst.

They showered together, taking their time soaping one another's bodies. Killian got on his knees in the tub and carefully washed her thighs and the hollows behind her knees, planting soft kisses on a spot near her hip.

"You've got four little freckles here," he said, looking up at her. "Like a constellation."

She smiled and ran her fingers through his hair as he brought his mouth back to the spot and connected the dots.

Later, they ordered pizza for dinner. The repairman Autumn had called showed up to install her new windows. The security system, complete with two surveillance cameras, would be installed the next day.

"I don't like the idea of leaving you here tonight without the security system," Killian said once the repairman left. "Maybe you should call Tana and ask her to come over."

"No, I'll be fine," she insisted. "I don't want to bother her. She's had a long day, covering for both of us at work."

Autumn had spoken to Tana after their shower, checking in as she'd promised she would. She could tell her friend was exhausted but was trying to hide it, asking if Autumn needed anything.

"I have everything I need right now," Autumn had assured her. "You get some rest and I'll see you in the morning."

"Are you sure you feel up to coming in? You don't have to."

"I'm not leaving you alone in the office for another day," Autumn had said firmly.

Killian looked as if he wanted to argue but was probably coming to the same conclusion she already had: with both Bill and Austin in jail, there was no threat to her for the moment. She would be safe at home until he returned.

When darkness had fallen over Pine Hollow like a blanket, Killian pulled his boots on and stood before her, velvety eyes holding so many words that his mouth couldn't form. She recognized *love* and *worry* and *fear* alongside the excitement he felt at finally getting close to finding what he was looking for.

"You be safe," she said, unable to keep the tremor from her voice. What he was doing was incredibly brave, exponentially dangerous. She knew she'd be a nervous wreck until he was back in her arms.

"Always," he said, and grabbed her by the waist, pulling her to him for a deep kiss.

Autumn watched him go with trepidation in her heart, keeping her eyes on his broad back until he disappeared into the shadows of the front yard.

Without Killian there to distract her, the thoughts she'd been avoiding all day came slamming into her. She sat down on the couch and turned on the television, tuned in to an old sitcom in the hopes that it would bring some comfort. Her mind kept going to Brooke, and she realized she'd never gone to visit like she had promised she would. Brooke was hurting, she was alone, and she couldn't even count on Autumn to keep her word.

The tears came with a vengeance, nearly choking her with their force, and Autumn let them. It was what she deserved, after all, for letting down a little girl who needed her. Misery cloaked her heart as she lay on the couch and let it consume her, thinking about all the things she'd done wrong lately. She fed it and fed it until she couldn't stand herself.

The only thing that helped in that state was another hot shower, so she went back upstairs and let the hot spray loosen the knots in her shoulders. She knew sleep wasn't going to come easy.

Killian was her comfort. His strong arms around her waist, full mouth on her throat, thick cock pushing against her, waiting to push everything else away. She braced herself with a hand against the shower wall and slid the other down over her belly, fingers working industriously as she imagined his tongue on her. He had a way of circling it around her clit, slowly, torturing her until she was on the brink of a scream, and she tried to mimic it the best she could. She came within a minute, shuddering in the hot spray of the shower, her knees weak.

After, she dressed in one of his old Metallica t-shirts—left slung over a chair in his hurry to leave—and a pair of black yoga pants, and brushed her fingers through her wet hair. If she had to endure the next several hours without Killian, at least she'd be enveloped in his scent.

The soft mewing of a cat jolted her from her thoughts and she moved to the window, peering through the curtains to see if a stray had wandered up onto the porch. It was too dark outside to make out much, but the sound was insistent. She got up, wiping her eyes with the sleeves of her sweatshirt, and looked through the glass panes on the front door. A tiny orange kitten, so small it could have fit in the palm of her hand, sat on the welcome mat. She pulled the door open and knelt to pick it up with a smile.

"Hey, buddy," she said. "Are you lost? You look a little young to be wandering around without your mama."

The kitten mewed pitifully. Autumn stood up with thoughts of getting a small saucer of milk from the kitchen, but before she could, a man stepped out of the shadows on the porch. He smiled, crooked teeth like gravestones between his lips, and held his hand up to his mouth palm-up. Autumn felt her eyes widen to the point of pain as he blew a bright blue powder into her face, recognition coming just a moment too late for her to run.

"The Bald Man?" Autumn whispered as the world swam around her. His smiling face was the last thing she saw as she slid to the floor unconscious.

***

Movement, smooth, like a boat gliding on water.

Autumn groaned softly, eyelids fluttering beneath shifting lights. After a few moments, she realized she was lying down in a moving car, passing beneath street lamps. A wave of nausea rolled through her and she put a hand to her head, trying to will the dizziness to go away. Briefly, she struggled to remember whose car she was in. Was Killian taking her to the hospital? No, she was fine, had rejected a trip to the E.R. when David asked. Memories passed through her mind as though she was flipping through photos in a book: Killian coming to her rescue, morphing from wolf to man; Austin holding her, bruising her; Bill's eyes gleaming in the moonlight as he ripped her shirt. She shuddered and struggled to sit up, but her body wouldn't obey.

Suddenly, she remembered the kitten, the Bald Man, the powder he'd blown into her eyes. The memory of her childhood nightmare crashed against the others and she nearly screamed, wanted to scream, but her throat felt locked. She was back in his car, and he was holding her captive. Autumn thought wildly of the doll, the ugly plastic baby with winky eyes. Eyes that could see her, the bald man had said in her memory, so he would know if she tried to escape.

"Well, hello," a voice said from in front of her. "Are you awake so soon?"

He sat in the driver's seat, only the top of his pale head visible to her as she lay motionless in the back. She imagined his claw-like hands gripping the steering wheel and nearly gagged in terror.

"I don't believe I ever introduced myself," he said, his voice crinkled like old paper. "My name is Ephraim Budd. We met long ago, do you remember? Oh, of course, you can't answer, but I doubt you have any memory of me. Our time together was cut frightfully short, unfortunately."

Autumn tried with all her strength to turn her head and was rewarded with a fraction of an inch, which only showed her more of the car's padded backrest. There was nothing around she could use as a weapon. She was without her coat or phone, and barefoot, so even if she did somehow get away, she'd tear up her feet doing it. Blind panic reared up in her chest and she tamped it down with a Herculean effort. She'd got away from this man once before when she was a child no older than Brooke. Surely she could do it again.

"This may seem scary, but I'm a *friend*," he said, stressing the last word as though she had argued with him. "I know all about you, Autumn, and you don't know much about me now, but you will."

The laugh that escaped him sounded like the scream of a steel door being thrown open and Autumn closed her eyes against it. She thought back to her nightmare, the one that had plagued her since she was a little girl. What details might she find there that would help her figure out what to do? She suddenly recalled Claire's words during her palm reading: *I see that you were taken as a child...Kidnapped. It's right here in the lines. See? This one deviates from the path, marking the time you spent away from your family. About a month, maybe more?*

Puzzle pieces were connecting, clicking together behind Autumn's eyes as the car's tires slid smoothly across the pavement beneath her. She saw what she had to do and honed her focus, pushing aside her fear so she could cast her mind outside of herself. Over the treetops, beneath cloudy skies. Toward Killian, who was running as a wolf across the landscape of Pine Hollow. She could almost see him in her mind's eye, a great beast running with the moon.

"It won't work," the Bald Man suddenly said with a gravelly laugh, and Autumn snapped her eyes open with a jolt. "Did you think I would allow you to travel? No, you'll have to settle for being trapped right here in your body, like your little friend."

Autumn felt a cold terror grip her stomach as she realized what he meant and heard a sob

escape her throat against her will.

"Don't worry, she's safe upfront with me," the Bald Man said, and she could hear the smile in his voice. "So pretty, she is, with all that pale blonde hair."

Chapter Eleven

Autumn wasn't sure when the car came to a stop. She might have been in the backseat for minutes or hours. The sky was still dark when she heard the squeal of brakes, and she wondered where Killian was.

Does he know I'm gone?

Whatever the Bald Man had used on her was still working; she couldn't move her limbs at all, could only turn her head a tiny bit from side to side.

Ephraim, she thought. *He said his name is Ephraim Budd. You have to remember that.*

The car dipped slightly as he got out of the front seat. Mumbled commands met her ears, but she couldn't hear clearly through the closed door. There was movement around the car, the sense things had been set into motion, and she pictured a throng of henchman eager to do the Bald Man's bidding. *Who was he?* she thought forcefully. Some sort of magician? The question of how he knew so much about her...how he knew about Brooke...gnawed at her insides until she felt sick.

The back door opened suddenly and a pair of hands wrapped a black sash around her eyes, knotting it behind her head. She could only lie prone and listen to the sound of her breathing as she was carried inside strong arms, away from the car and across a field. Crickets chirped their reedy night music as the cold night air hit her skin, and she smelled wet grass and the wild, alarming scent of large animals. Moments later, she felt a rush of warm air and knew she'd been taken inside a building. She was placed on something soft, sitting up, but her hands and feet were quickly bound with a thick cloth.

"Careful, now," said Ephraim Budd. His strange, high-pitched voice was as grating on her ears like nails on a chalkboard. "Don't hurt her."

Autumn's fingers tingled as relief coursed through her body, leaving her legs weak. Whatever the Bald Man had blown in her face had only briefly paralyzed her, and it was wearing off. She was careful to give no sign, keeping her hands as still as possible.

Somewhere on her, left a heavy door banged shut, leaving the room uncomfortably silent. She could still feel a presence around her and fought the urge to cover her face, afraid of an attack of some kind.

"I know this all seems very unfair," Ephraim said suddenly. He was much closer than Autumn had realized. His breath smelled like rotting meat. Her heart thumped madly as she did her best to keep from leaning away from him, and she realized that was the point. He was trying to trick her into giving away how much mobility she had. "But I wouldn't have brought you here unless it was absolutely necessary."

Behind the blindfold, she closed her eyes and focused on Killian's face to find a measure of calm, wishing she had the strength to overcome her mind's inability to let her travel. Whatever he'd given her was powerful, and she felt a stabbing pain in her stomach as she realized he'd probably given it to Brooke, too. There were cold fingers against her cheek, a nudge, then the blindfold was lifted. The Bald Man's face hovered before her as he bent to meet her eye line. She suppressed a shudder; he was nearly unchanged from her memory of him, although he was almost 30 years older.

"*Do* you remember me, dear?" he asked. His tongue, thick as an infected worm, snaked out from between cracked lips. "I could have sworn I saw something in your eyes when you opened the door."

She sat completely still, watching him in silence. Behind him, she could see a small glimpse of the room she was in. It was a basement of some kind, with leather couches along the far wall and recessed lighting that had been dimmed considerably. Knowing that might work in her favor, she wriggled her fingers the tiniest bit against her stomach, testing the bonds that had been tied around her wrists. It was a cloth of some kind, wrapped tightly and knotted. She assumed her ankles were bound with the same material.

"Hmm," he murmured, narrowing his eyes at her shrewdly. "You never were much of a talker."

Autumn watched as he sat back in a chair across from her, moving slowly as though he was in pain. *Good*, she thought, *I hope you are. I hope you're falling apart.*

"I'm sure you're wondering why you're here," Ephraim said. "Some associates of mine were afraid you were getting too close to a secret they've worked hard to keep. They recently took the initiative to enter your home while you were out to try and find out how much you knew."

Bill and Austin. Autumn's stomach clenched in revulsion as she pictured them rifling through her things, not just breaking and destroying but touching and seeking.

"Fortunately for me, they placed a listening device inside your bedroom while they were there," Ephraim said, his livery lips spreading in a slow smile. "We've heard some interesting things, Miss Phillips. Stories a less enlightened person might dismiss as fantasy, but which I understood to be the truth. Werewolves and astral projection and...well, there might have been more had there not been lots of distractions in the form of physical love. That part my associates found particularly engaging."

Heat rose in Autumn's face. Her breathing quickened as she fought the urge to lash out and claw the disgusting old man's eyes with her fingernails. He watched her carefully. She knew he was baiting her, trying to get a rise.

Her mind raced with the news that the Napiers knew about her abilities, that they knew what Killian was. What did Ephraim Budd want with that information? Autumn felt like a fool. She had foolishly poured her heart out to Killian about Brooke, and now the little girl had been kidnapped because of it. If only she'd kept her mouth shut.

Ephraim stood slowly and walked closer to her, stooped over in an old man's gait.

"You're going to help me find someone very dear to me," he said.

He reached out to stroke her cheek and she saw her chance. With as much strength as she could muster, Autumn reared back and headbutted him so hard she saw stars. He grunted and went down with no grace, crumpling to the floor like a pile of rags.

Wasting no time, she got to work twisting her hands inside their binding, pulling and yanking until the fabric was stretched just enough for her to get free. In a few moments, she'd undone the binds at her ankles and cautiously stood up on tingly bare feet. Pins and needles prickled beneath her skin and she grimaced, hobbling over to the door. There was no way to know who or what might be guarding it from the outside, but she had to take the chance and run. Autumn pushed open the heavy oak door and peeked out, expecting to see a werewolf racing toward her across the field.

What she didn't expect to see was her father standing there with his arms crossed.

I know that deep down, you understand that you're not free of him, even though you tell yourself often that you are, Claire whispered in her mind. *There has always been the possibility that he would come back into your life.*

***

Autumn was dreaming, but not traveling.

Killian stood at the mouth of the quarry with his back to her, strong hands at his sides. A fine mist crept up behind him in the grass, stealthy as a snake. It made her uneasy, so she walked forward. Her feet felt stuck in molasses and she looked down to see thick mud crawling up around her ankles. It sucked at her boots with every step.

"Killian?" she said softly. "It's okay."

He shook his head. "It's not okay. I failed."

"You didn't," she said. Walking was becoming harder with every movement. If she stood still, she sank a quarter of an inch into the earth. "I'm the one who failed. I couldn't keep Brooke safe and now they have her."

He bowed his head, shoulders rounded in defeat. She wanted to run to him, to wrap her arms around his waist and show him that everything would be alright, but she couldn't escape the ground. The mud had grown tendrils like vines that wound up her legs, trying to keep her in place.

Killian turned to face her with tears streaming down his face, but they were made of blood. Crimson rivulets coursed down his cheeks as he took a step backward.

"I can't stay," he said. "I'm sorry."

"Killian, NO," Autumn screamed, reaching for him, but she was too far away and the vines were insidious. They reached to her hips, dragging her down, and she fell to her knees just as Killian stepped off the edge of the cliff.

Autumn flailed awake, hands punching the air as she tried to claw her way to the surface of the dream. A cry escaped her and she forced her eyes open, afraid of what she might see behind her eyelids if she left them closed.

"Look who's joined us again," Ephraim said, his grating voice like a buzzsaw in the near dark. "Were you dreaming of the one who got away?"

Autumn rolled onto her side and clutched her stomach, feeling like she might be sick. She was back in the basement room, and Ephraim was watching her from his place on the couch. Behind him, she spied something she had failed to notice before: framed family photographs. Bill and Austin Napier stood in most of them, smiling on the golf course or opening Christmas gifts with their parents. She was in their home, on their turf.

"What did you do to me?" she groaned. Her last clear memory was of seeing her father as she made her escape and she jerked convulsively at the image of his face. It had been over a decade since she'd seen him, but he still looked the same.

"The question is, what did you do to *me*?" he said, rubbing his head. A large, dark bruise had already spread there like a stain. "You were trying to leave the party before it'd even begun, and that won't do," Ephraim said, choking out a laugh.

She cringed at the sound; her head felt like it might split open at any moment. She thought wildly of the myth of Zeus and his massive headache, from which his daughter Athena sprang fully-formed. *If only a goddess were around now*, she thought.

"I had to give you a little something to keep you here," Ephraim went on. "Only a little sleeping elixir."

"And what did you give me at my house?" she asked, pushing herself up on her hands and knees with effort. Her legs felt wobbly. "The stuff you blew in my face, was that a drug?"

"A cocktail I've been working on for a few years now," he said. "I'm something of a chemist, you see. It might be of great interest to you to know my field of expertise is dream suppression, although I dabble in other things as well. For instance, I've created a tincture that alters the gene sequence responsible for a werewolf's transformation. That was one of my prouder moments because it brought your father and me together."

Autumn frowned and brought a hand to her head, suddenly woozy. Unable to stand after all, she dropped back to the floor and tried to keep the world from spinning. It was so difficult to focus on what he was saying, like trying to hear someone speak underwater.

"What? What does my father have to do with werewolves?"

"Only everything," Roland Phillips said, stepping out from the shadows to stand before her. She looked up at him and in her state he seemed impossibly tall, towering over her with his muscular forearms crossed. "It was my idea. They're pretty useful things to have around, turns out."

"You're the kingpin," she whispered. "I thought it was Michael Napier but all this time, it was you."

"Kingpin," her father said, rolling the word around in his mouth. Tasting it. "I like that."

He laughed and Ephraim joined him. Autumn covered her ears with both hands, wishing she could vomit and feel better, get it over with. The news her father was the one Killian had been looking for nearly turned her inside out. She scooted backward to get away from him and pressed her back against the nearest wall so she could keep an eye on both him and Ephraim at the same time.

"I do remember you," she said to Ephraim. "I dream about you sometimes, about the night you took me."

"Marvelous," Ephraim exclaimed, clapping his hands. "I was so afraid I hadn't left an impression on you. Seven years old, you were, just a tiny little thing."

"You stole me from my parents and terrorized me with a doll," she spat. "You told me she watched everything I did, that she would let you know if I tried to escape."

"Well, I had to keep you in line somehow," Ephraim said. "I couldn't use the suppression drug on you because I needed you to be able to travel. And as far as stealing you...I'm afraid you've got it all wrong, dear. Your father permitted me to take you."

She looked at her father, who still stood with his arms crossed, a smug expression on his face.

"You let him kidnap me?" she asked, suddenly feeling short of breath. It made a strange kind of sense. No wonder her parents had never spoken of it. She felt a mixture of anger and resentment surge through her dreamy nausea at the idea that her mother might have known, as well. "You…gave me away?"

"Don't be so dramatic," her father said, narrowing his eyes contemptuously. "I let him take you for a while so you could help him. Your mother was in the hospital, she never even knew you were gone."

"Help him with what?" she asked through clenched teeth.

Ephraim cleared his throat and leaned forward on the couch. "You don't remember her? My Catherine?"

Autumn shook her head with a frown, but there *was* something at the sound of that name, a spark of recognition. She searched her memories but found nothing there to help her bring it to the surface.

"My granddaughter," Ephraim said. "A beautiful angel, a perfect little blonde seraph. She had talents much like yours, Autumn. She traveled when she slept. I never knew, of course, until one night when she fell asleep and didn't come back. Her body lived on, still breathed and pumped blood, but her spirit was lost. I brought in every healer I could find, five psychics, a team of doctors. The doctors were baffled and suggested a bacterial infection which had likely put her into a coma. The healers said I should anoint her body with oils and pray for her safe return. The psychics, though, all told me the same thing: she had traveled too far from her body and had gotten lost. My only hope was to find another traveler who might be able to connect with her and bring her home."

Autumn suddenly remembered a dream in which she spoke with a little blonde girl, a Brooke-lookalike. She'd thought at the time that it was simply her mind's way of coping with the news of Tommy's death and the realization that she would have to figure out how to help Brooke, but that hadn't been it at all. For whatever reason, her dreaming mind had pushed the Bald Man to the forefront, and then it had progressed naturally to his granddaughter. Catherine.

"I've been keeping her body alive all these years," Ephraim said, his voice trembling like a leaf in the wind. "At home, in her bed. She has a team of caregivers that make sure she gets the nutrition she needs, that she's turned to prevent bedsores. But tonight, she's here. Tonight, she comes home to her body. And when that happens, she'll be able to heal quickly, because now I have the medicine to keep her from traveling again. She'll finally be safe."

Autumn imagined the old man living in a run-down mansion, keeping his granddaughter alive on machines as time marched on and crumbled everything around them, and nearly gagged with the sheer horror of it.

"You found her," Ephraim said softly. "About four weeks after I brought you to my home, you found her in the woods, but she wouldn't come with you."

Flashes of the bedroom she'd slept in...a four-poster bed with dark curtains drawn around it to block the light...popped in her brain like camera shutter clicks and she recoiled from them. He had made her sleep beside Catherine's body, she recalled with a shudder when she was traveling.

"I tried," she said as those days resurfaced. "She was scared. I tried to get her to follow me back."

"But you couldn't," Ephraim said. "And then your mother died and you had to go home. I asked your father to keep an eye on you after that, to see if you were still traveling, but it was as I'd feared; the trauma you experienced after the loss of your mother kept you in place when you slept. You forgot all about your abilities, kept them locked away in some dark little corner of your mind. And with them went the memory of my Catherine."

Autumn saw her father in her mind's eye, sitting in her bedroom in the dark with a gun across his lap.

"You were scared of me," she said to her father quietly. "I never understood it back then, why you did the things you did, but it's so clear now. It's why you let me go so easily when I told you I wanted to move out. You were glad to see me go."

"I'm not scared of anything," Roland said, his voice a taut tightrope she couldn't walk across. "But I *was* glad to see you go. I had things I wanted to do. Ephraim here owed me big, said he had a solution to a problem of mine. I had a little business when your mother was alive, but it was nothing like what it could have been. I didn't have the manpower, couldn't find people I trusted to guard what I'd built."

Autumn recalled the night in her childhood that had been etched into memory; the night her father had shot a man in their front yard. He'd been in the drug business even then, she realized.

"So you stole people who had the power to transform," Autumn said, shaking her head in disgust. "You gave them a drug to keep them from changing so they would do your bidding. You're fucking sick."

"Nah," Roland said, baring his teeth in a slow smile. "I'm a businessman."

"A little monkshood is all it takes to keep them in line," Ephraim said. "Not inhumane, really. We even let them out to hunt on occasion, although I had to develop an elixir that would ensure their quick return. In my work, I've found ways to change man to beast and back again, to bring about rage when it is required, to help someone sleep, to keep their souls in place. Some might think me a god, you know, but It's all in the chemistry."

"Not inhumane? Keeping a werewolf from transforming puts their body into a permanent state of pain and decay," Autumn said. "You're not a god. You're monsters, both of you."

"Monsters?" Ephraim repeated thoughtfully. "No, I don't think so. I've been extremely kind to your little friend. She's upstairs right now, sleeping peacefully beside my Catherine. She has every comfort imaginable."

A painful cramp tore through Autumn's stomach and she doubled over. *Brooke*, she thought, eyes squeezed tightly against the pain.

"If she was all you wanted, why did you take me?" she groaned, rolling over onto her hands and knees. Her sweat-dampened hair hung in her face like a curtain.

"Oh, my dear," Ephraim said, standing slowly from the couch. He walked closer to Roland and they looked down at her with identical smiles, as though they'd gotten away with something. "Haven't you figured it out by now? You're the bait."

The pain in her abdomen tripled and Autumn screamed, writhing in agony. It shot out in a million different directions throughout her body, a feeling like knives in her bloodstream, from her stomach to her fingertips. She held her hand up to her face and watched in terror as her fingers elongated, stretching past the point of pain and onto another plane of suffering altogether. Her feet began the same torturous change: free of shoes, they were pulled and extended before her eyes. Coarse, reddish hair sprouted from her pores, her senses heightened almost cruelly. She could smell the sweat and blood of the two men before her, the verdant grass outside the door, the droppings of the animals who were being kept captive elsewhere on the property.

She lay panting on the floor, no longer Autumn but something else, something *evolved*. An image crowded into her mind: a butterfly emerging from a cocoon.

And as she smelled a different, more familiar scent approaching stealthily outside, the beast that had once been Autumn staggered to its feet, trying to form a word. There was no language left, though, only a vague memory of a name and the feeling of being loved. A cage made of two strong arms.

"Do your worst," Ephraim said and blew a burst of red powder into the beast's eyes.

Chapter Twelve

The moon was bright and clear, and the beast had an empty belly.

She moved silently across the field, keeping her massive head low, nostrils flaring to delicately test the air. The familiar scent was close. Images flashed through her mind: a splash of red against green, a curved road, a forest dappled in the early morning sunlight. These were things she recognized, but faintly, as though they were viewed through a fog. There was a feeling, too, a curious one that left her wishing she could curl up in a warm place and sleep: comfort.

Yet Master had given clear instructions: *Do your worst*. She had breathed in his reddish powder and felt simple, clean rage envelop her, the kind that came with torn throats. She did not wish to anger Master, and what he wanted was a fight. She was strong, muscles tensed and ready, long legs prepared to spring. Across the landscape, shadows moved in as clouds rolled across the moon.

She would have to rely on her other senses, and she knew they would serve her well.

The wind rushed up into the trees, rattling the leaves with a sound like an ocean wave crashing on the shore. She sat perfectly still and surveyed the hills, waiting for a signal. After several long moments, an oily shadow moved away from the fence at the bottom of the valley and darted toward a tree. She kept her eyes on it and crept to the left, moving like inky silk in the dark.

It was him. A black wolf with the scent of a man, golden eyes glimmering even from a distance. She stopped moving and changed direction, circling back to take cover behind a tree as he moved quietly up the hill toward the house.

He hadn't seen her. She waited until he moved to within ten feet, and then his eyes widened as he caught her scent on the wind. She sprang from the shadows, claws out.

He saw her at the last moment and rolled to the right. She went sprawling in the grass and doubled back, slipping a bit in the dew. He was already standing on his hind legs, waiting for her next move, and when she dove in the air toward him he batted her away with one powerful paw.

She landed hard and turned around, panting. The anger that bubbled in her veins was close to boiling over and she kept an image of Master in her head as motivation. This wolf was much stronger than she was, much older. They circled one another, restless, and sprang at the same time. He pushed her to the ground and held her there with his front paws, snarling, teeth gleaming in the dim light. She snapped fiercely at him but couldn't make a connection as he darted away. He was playing with her.

With a great roar of rage, she leaped from the ground and jumped on his back as he walked away, sinking her teeth into the dense fur at the back of his neck. Blood flooded her mouth, red and mercurial. Howling in pain and surprise, he reared back like a stallion and flung her off, swatting with his claws at the same time. They swiped her side and she felt the high, silvery pain immediately.

The other wolf landed on all fours and tensed low to the ground, ready to spring again, but stopped when the scent of her blood hit him. His snout tilted into the air for a moment, sniffing, and his eyes widened in recognition.

She lay on her side, panting, wounded, weakened. Watching as the black wolf padded slowly over and nudged her shoulder, whining. The familiarity was still there, prickling the back of her mind, and she opened herself up to it for a moment instead of pushing it away. The seeds of memory were pushed down deep in the soil of her mind, but they were accessible. They had grown roots. She recalled a voice comforting her, a man who looked fierce but was gentle. The first one to bring about a change for the better in her, to recognize the strength that lived in her bones. The only one to see a light in her darkness.

She looked up at the moon as it threw off the last of the clouds and felt a change beginning, a transformation that began in the pit of her stomach and radiated outward. The black wolf watched with wide eyes as she reversed what had been done to her with the aid of the moon, drawing it into her body and feeding on its strength. When she lay naked and trembling and human once more, she reached a hand up to touch the black wolf's mane, mindful of the wounds she had given him. Her injury had already begun to close up, but the lacerations were deep and would take time to fully heal.

"Killian?" she whispered.

"Gotcha," said a voice from behind her, and a steel collar was thrown over the black wolf's head and secured by a firm wire lead.

Killian howled and bucked, jumping several feet off the ground to escape the contraption, but it was no use. Roland was strong, and he had the upper hand. Bill and Austin stood on either side of him, each holding a branch of the lead. As Autumn watched, Roland threw a handful of powder into Killian's face and she knew with sudden clarity it was the concoction Ephraim had created to keep the wolves from changing back into their human form.

"Killian," Autumn screamed as firm hands reached beneath her arms and hauled her backward through the grass. She kicked and twisted her body and managed to gain the upper hand, flipping away and pulling herself onto her feet. Panting, exhausted, she slowly stood up and stared hard at Ephraim, uncaring that she was nude.

"How are you so strong?" she asked, teeth clenched. "Why are you unchanged after almost thirty years?"

"It's a simple trick of alchemy," he said with an infuriating smile. "I could teach you, you know. Wouldn't you love to lengthen your life? To know that each day is worth so much more because you can truly take your time and enjoy it?"

Autumn shook her head. "You're messing with the laws of nature, and it's going to catch up to you."

"Oh, but I have so many tricks up my sleeve," Ephraim said. "You wouldn't believe how many."

Lightning-fast, he pulled his hand from his pocket and prepared to blow the blue sleeping powder into her face, but Autumn was quick, too. She whipped out her arm and smacked his hand away so that the powder flew into his face. Ephraim stumbled backward, eyes wide, staring at her in disbelief.

"I'm familiar with your tricks," she said as he fell unceremoniously to the ground.

Even wounded, even in her unabashed nudity, Autumn suddenly felt extremely powerful. With the moonlight on her shoulders and the fall air in her nose, she walked purposefully toward the house.

The sound of Killian's tormented howls chilled her to the bone, but she forced herself to stand tall as she made her way inside.

"Well, look who it is," Bill said as she entered the basement. He stood with Austin over an anguished and ferocious Killian, whose teeth were bared and gleaming in the dim light. Roland was nowhere to be seen. "You come back to party?"

His eyes roved over her bare body; she felt Austin's gaze too, searing across her skin, and remembered that they'd been in her home. Searching through her things. Did they look through her underwear drawer? Steal a little something for themselves for later? She smirked at the thought of it, at how pathetic they were.

"Yes," she said. "I did come to party."

She moved closer, holding up a hand to still Killian. Keeping Bill's gaze in her own, she smiled as sweetly as she could manage and ran a soft finger down the front of his shirt.

"You know I always liked you," she said. "It's a shame we had to let all this silly business come between us. We could have been something good."

He let out a breath and shot a look at Austin. "Well, we don't have to be enemies. If you're ready to talk things out, we can go upstairs."

"Sounds good," she whispered.

"Hey," Austin said. "She's hurt."

Bill looked down at her side, where Killian's claws had torn open a gash on her ribcage. The wound was still stitching itself together and had left behind a violent purple swath of bruised skin around it.

"Don't worry," she said. "I can barely feel it."

It was exactly the distraction she needed. As soon as Bill looked down, he loosened his grip on the lead and Killian leaped forward, swiping Bill's face with claws extended and a roar that blew her hair back. Certain that Killian could hold his own, Autumn ducked out of the way and ran for the staircase to search for Brooke.

She'd never been inside the Napier's mansion before, but it was much as she had pictured it: long, wide hallways, lush floral wallpaper, mahogany furniture. She passed a library that boasted bookshelves from floor to ceiling and a massive game room complete with billiards and air hockey tables. There were many more closed doors than she would have liked; the urgency was quite real now. She could hear Killian and the boys fighting downstairs and moved quickly but silently through the dim passageways, stopping only when she saw an open bedroom that offered a plush bathrobe hanging on the door. She swiped it and threw it around her body, knotting the belt around her waist.

On the third floor, only one door was open. Guided by the moonlight streaming in through the windows, Autumn walked forward and saw a massive bed that dominated the room; on it sat Brooke, who was awake and speaking quietly to a woman laying hooked up to machines.

"Autumn," Brooke cried, jumping down from the bed to run to her. "You came. I tried to find you while I was asleep, but you were gone. This is my friend Catherine. She's real tired. I found her while I was looking for you."

Autumn picked Brooke up and held her tight, feeling tears fill her eyes as she breathed in the little girl's baby shampoo-scent. She cradled Brooke's head with her hand and looked at her closely, checking her for marks.

"Are you okay? Did they hurt you?" she asked.

"Who?" Brooke asked, tilting her head curiously.

"Never mind," Autumn said, smiling past the lump in her throat.

"I'm sorry I traveled," Brooke said, twirling Autumn's hair between her fingers. "I know you told me not to, but I couldn't help it."

"It's okay, Bee," Autumn said.

She moved slowly to the side of the bed, where Catherine lay prone. Too weak to move much more than her eyes, she followed Autumn's movement with curiosity.

"I'm sure you don't remember me," Autumn said. "We met a long time ago. I tried to find you and bring you home, but I failed. Brooke here is a hero, and we're going to take good care of you, okay?"

Catherine nodded, her pale lips curving into a smile. All the time away from her body had taken a toll. Half of her dark blonde hair was grey, and there were considerable lines on her face from the stress and pain of being bedridden for so long.

"Where's Uncle Bill?" Brooke asked with a yawn. "He told me if I was real good and stayed in bed, he'd let me play with his dogs."

Bill and Austin must have busted out of jail and taken Brooke from her home. Autumn shuddered as she realized what they'd probably done to the state worker who had been assigned to care for her.

"Uncle Bill is...busy," Autumn said, lowering Brooke gently to the floor. So far, this end of the house was silent, and that worried her. "Listen, Bee, I need you to try and remember for me. What else did Uncle Bill tell you?"

"He said to look for Catherine while I was asleep because she was lost, and he said if I found her he'd buy me a puppy to keep."

"Oh yeah?" Autumn asked, forcing a smile. "Listen, I need you to do something for me. Can you be a big girl and do as I say?"

Brooke nodded.

"I'm going to leave the room, and when I do, I want you to lock the door behind me and don't open it for any reason, for anyone unless it's me. Can you do that?"

"But why?" Brooke asked, pouting. "I want to go with you."

"I know, Bee, and I'm going to take you with me soon, but first I have to do something, and I need to know that you'll be safe in here with Catherine."

"Okay," Brooke said, but she wasn't happy about it.

Autumn kissed her cheek and left the room, closing the door behind her. She waited a beat until she heard the lock click, then crept down the hallway with one arm wrapped around her midsection. The plan had been to check the floor for signs of anyone else, but the more she moved, the more her wounds felt like they were opening back up.

Unwrapping the robe, she sucked a breath in through her teeth seeing the massive bruise that dominated her torso. It ran the length of her side, around the claw marks, and up to her shoulder blade. She gingerly touched the wound and winced. It hadn't opened as she'd thought, but it was definitely in need of some care.

Other, older bruises dotted her other side and she frowned, trying to remember where they'd come from. The memory of her run-in with Bill and Austin in the woods hit her, as well as a thought she'd had afterward: that Austin must have superhuman strength to have done so much damage with only his arms.

Her eyes widened as she realized what it meant and she thrust the robe closed, running at top speed despite her pain. She tore down the hallway, down a flight of stairs, across another corridor, and down into the basement, where Killian was still locked in battle with Bill and Austin.

She was too late.

The brothers had already transformed into wolves and were tearing up the basement during their assault on Killian, destroying furniture and smashing photos off the wall as they reared back and swiped at him with claws out. She watched helplessly for a moment, unable to contain a scream as one of them tossed Killian into a wall and sent a huge, heavy, gilt-frame mirror crashing to the ground. It broke into a million pieces, sending glass flying in murderous shards all around the room.

For the moment, the back door was unguarded. She ran for it, slamming the door open and sprinting into the cold night air. She ran down the hill, eyes scanning the shadowy grass for a lump, and nearly cried out with relief when she saw it. Ephraim.

He was still out cold, lying on his side with one arm bent beneath him at an odd angle. She ran to him and tore his jacket open, searching frantically inside the pockets and sleeves for the array of powders she knew he kept there. Deep down in the inner breast pocket, she found several small plastic bags full of his elixirs and pulled them out with a cry of triumph. The problem was that she didn't know which one did what.

Autumn sat back on her heels in the cold grass and cast her mind out for a moment, trying hard to recall the moment when her father had first captured Killian in front of her. He'd thrown powder into Killian's face— what color had it been? Blue was for sleeping, she knew, and the red stuff had briefly allowed her to transform. That left yellow and purple, and she was sure it hadn't been yellow. She grabbed two of the purple bags and one blue and ran back up the hill, pushing away her exhaustion to find an inner strength she didn't even know she had.

"Killian," she screamed as she ran inside the basement.

The fighting ceased immediately and all three wolves turned to look at her, bloodied and fatigued, panting with exertion. The largest—Autumn suspected it was Austin—pulled back its snout and bared its teeth at her, a low growl rumbling in the back of its throat.

"Not today," Autumn said tiredly and opened her palm.

Filling her lungs with as much breath as she could gather, she blew the purple dust directly into their faces and watched as the transformation began, a painful morphing process that made her wince as limbs shortened and bones cracked. All three men writhed on the floor in agony. When the change was complete, they lay still for a long moment, glistening with sweat and blood.

Autumn walked calmly to Bill and Austin, standing over them with a look of disgust on her face.

"How dare you," she said softly. She thought of all the things they'd done, all the ways they'd tried to hurt her, and felt a cold rage throbbing inside her ribcage.

"This ain't over," Bill said weakly, rolling onto his side with a grunt of effort.

"That's where you're wrong," said Autumn, and tossed the blue powder into his face before moving on to Austin. They were unconscious within moments.

On the other side of the room, Killian still lay naked, bloodied, and panting from the fight. He pulled himself to a shaky standing position and walked to Autumn, tears filling his eyes as he brought both hands up to her face.

"My God," he sobbed. "I nearly killed you. I'm so sorry, Autumn. I've failed you."

"Yes, you didn't quite get the job done, did you?" came a cruel voice from behind him.

Autumn looked up to see her father standing in the doorway. He had a gun pointed directly at the back of Killian's head.

"It was an easy job, or it should've been for someone like you," said Roland. "She ain't nothin' but a little slip of a girl, not a threat at all, and you still fucked it up."

Time seemed to slow. Autumn recalled her dream of Killian jumping from the cliff over the quarry, the bloody tears streaming down his face as he apologized to her. She looked into his eyes and smiled.

"You didn't fail me," she said softly and used the last of her strength to twist her body around his.

She heard the gunshot, as loud as cannon fire, heard Killian's roar as he realized what she'd done. She waited for the impact of the bullet, braced herself for the pain.

But no pain came. Instead, there was a shattering sound and she turned to the right to see a vase explode into a thousand fragile splinters of porcelain. Dozens of red flowers burst into fragments and rained down around them as Roland screamed something unintelligible. Autumn spun around to find a massive grey wolf had jumped on him and clamped its teeth into his shoulder, throwing the shot wild. Her father went down into the grass with a thud.

One of the captive wolves, Autumn thought distantly. Likely it had escaped from wherever Bill and Austin were holding it, because of all the commotion outside.

"Here," she said, holding out her hand to the wolf. In her palm lay the other bag of purple powder. "Take this to the others so they can cycle. Hurry, it's twenty minutes 'til midnight."

The wolf padded over and pulled the packet gently from her hand with its mouth, amber eyes seeming to flash with gratitude as it turned and loped away.

Autumn looked up dreamily at the red petals floating down upon their heads and began to laugh, clinging to Killian as he wrapped his strong arms around her waist and pulled her to him. She had remembered Brooke's warning to her after a nightmare, one that didn't make sense at the time:

Stay away from the roses.

Epilogue

3 Weeks Later

Autumn and Killian sat on a picnic blanket near the quarry, letting the warm sun shine down on their shoulders.

Brooke sat on her blanket nearby, having a tea party with her dolls. Autumn watched her with a smile, marveling at how strong the little girl was. Since the loss of her mother and the kidnapping, she hadn't shown any signs of regression and was doing well with her foster family. Autumn had appealed to the judge to be allowed to remain Brooke's caseworker for the time being, and given all the child had been through, he'd approved it.

"I love watching you with her," Killian said, stroking Autumn's cheek gently. "You're completely in your element."

She smiled. "She makes it easy. I love that kid."

"She loves you, too. And she's not the only one."

Autumn leaned forward and kissed him, keeping it quick and light since Brooke was nearby.

"Have you heard from any of the pack?" she asked softly.

Killian's eyes darkened the tiniest bit. Talking about that night was difficult for him, in more ways than one. Autumn knew he felt like a failure because he couldn't keep her safe, and every time she undressed he saw the evidence of what he'd done: four long slashes across her ribcage. He'd had long, sleepless nights because of it. No matter what she said to ease his mind, he couldn't get past her scars or his guilt.

"I spoke to James, the grey wolf who helped us," Killian said. "He said that once the ones who were being held captive cycled, they turned on Roland immediately and carried him off into the woods. I wouldn't like to think about how things ended for him."

Autumn sat silently with that for a long moment. Roland hadn't been a father to her, not truly, but it was still strange to think about where his fate had ended up. She shivered despite the warmth of the sun and looked out over the cliff, where the trees across the quarry were flame-colored in their death throes.

Bill and Austin Napier were in jail awaiting transfer to a state prison, where they would stay until their trial. David had booked them on three charges of kidnapping—for herself, Killian, and Brooke—-and six felony charges related to drugs, as well as murder in the first degree for the killing of Janet Warren, the state worker who'd been assigned to care for Brooke. Autumn recalled her realization that they had been taking doses of Ephraim's elixir to become full-fledged werewolves, irritated that she hadn't seen it before. Their inhuman strength, particularly evident during the fight with Killian in the woods, should have tipped her off, but her mind had been on other things.

The Napier compound, as it was being called in the local news, had hidden vast underground labs full of homegrown poppies and marijuana plants, as well as areas for packing and shipping. They both tried to pin the blame on Roland, immediately giving him up for his role

in the drug dynasty, and his home was promptly raided. Police found enough evidence there to put him away for life. He was nowhere to be found, of course. Michael Napier was also missing, although no one had taken credit for that one yet.

Ephraim Budd had been remanded to the care of the state after officers found him deliriously wandering around the Napier property, babbling nonsense about a girl coming back into her body after a long journey. The judge sent him for a lengthy stay at a mental health facility with bars on the windows. Catherine, meanwhile, had no memory of what had happened to her, but her caregivers told police all they needed to know: that she'd been in a coma and was extremely ill, but seemed to be on the mend. With no one else to take on the role, she'd been named executor of Ephraim's estate because she'd been designated as such in his will. In the chaos of the investigation, David hadn't asked why Catherine was at the Napiers', and Autumn hadn't volunteered a guess, claiming ignorance. There were already too many questions with no easy answers.

As far as the police were concerned, Bill and Austin had kidnapped Brooke, Autumn, and Killian with the aid of drugs, and when Killian came to, a fight ensued. Their previous bad blood played a big role in selling the story. Autumn spun it to David as a tale of revenge gone wrong.

Of course, Autumn knew Tana was going to be a little harder to convince than David, and she wanted to be honest. As soon as they'd been released from the Napiers', Autumn called her best friend and asked her to come over. They sat in her living room with Killian and Autumn shared the story haltingly, afraid of how Tana might react to the news that he was a werewolf. But in true Tana form, she'd taken it in stride and had even got in touch with Claire, who was working with Brooke once a week to help her control her sleep travels. The fact that Brooke had also shown evidence of psychic talent was not lost on Claire, and although Autumn was glad Brooke had someone to help her through it all, she was also that much more worried for the girl. It was going to be a long road to true recovery as she learned how to balance and control her mind.

"What do you think happened to all the drugs Ephraim made?" Autumn asked. "Are they still out there in the world, ready to hurt people?"

Killian shook his head. "The pack sniffed out his house, found his lab. They burned it to the ground before the cops could get to it."

"Well, that's a relief, at least," Autumn said. "You know, as evil as that man is, I'm grateful he gave me the gift of transformation. In my brief time as a werewolf, I learned a few things."

"Oh yeah?" he asked. There was a sadness in his eyes at the memory and she was sorry for it, but it was also something she needed to talk about.

"I'm stronger than I give myself credit for," she explained. "My dad kind of beat that out of me, so to speak. Not with his fists, but mentally and emotionally, and that was almost worse."

"I already knew you were strong," Killian said, smiling a little.

"Yeah, but I didn't. I think it took something huge for me to learn."

"Autumn, there's something we haven't talked about."

She looked up at him expectantly. "If this is about our fight..."

"No," he said quickly, bringing her hand up to his mouth to kiss it. "I...you almost took a bullet for me. You could have died."

"Yes...?"

"Well don't get me wrong, I'm eternally grateful, but why on earth would you do that?"

She bit her lip, trying to think of the best way to answer. In the end, it all came down to a simple idea.

"I had a dream about you after Ephraim took me," she said. "I dreamed that you jumped off that cliff over there because you couldn't live with the thought you'd failed me in some way. When I realized what my father was going to do...when I saw that gun in his hand...I thought of the dream and knew I could never let you think that. I thought, *Even if I die, at least he'll see what he did for me*."

Killian frowned. "I don't understand. What did I do for you?"

She leaned forward and touched his face lightly, cupping her hand around his jaw. "You taught me I'm more than what I've been told. You loved me without asking for anything in return. If you hadn't done those things, I never would have made it through that night. I never would have had the courage to put myself between you and that gun."

He blinked and swiped a hand across his eyes and she knew he was shaken by her words.

"Well don't ever do it again, okay?" he said, and she laughed.

"I'm not making any promises."

They sat in comfortable silence for a moment, watching Brooke play, and then Killian turned to her.

"It's almost Halloween."

She smiled. "Yes, it is. I've already got my costume all planned out."

"Oh yeah? Are we having a party?"

"*We*? Have you decided to move in?" she teased. Killian had all but done that already.

"Well, I thought since it's your favorite time of year and everything, maybe we could do something special."

He pulled a tiny, blue velvet box from his pocket and placed it on the blanket between them. Autumn looked down at it, feeling her heart speed up until it was trip hammering in her chest.

"Is that what I think it is?"

Killian leaned forward and kissed her gently, then pulled back to look into her eyes.

"Only if you're ready for it," he said.

It's only been a month, a voice whispered in her mind. *You can't possibly be ready for this.*

But she hadn't been ready for anything that happened three weeks ago: she hadn't been prepared for a second kidnapping, for her soul to leave her body, for her father to come roaring back into her life only to try and rip it to shreds.

But she'd come through it to the other side a stronger, more capable person.

"I am," she said softly, and her smile felt truly authentic for the first time in weeks. "I'm ready."

ABOUT THE AUTHOR

Amanda is a writer and artist whose short fiction has been published in *Barren Magazine, Eastern Iowa Review, The Hellebore,* and more. She is the author of the middle grade fiction novel, and her horror poetry, *Tall Grass,* and *The Day You Learned To Swim,* both made the shortlist for Bram Stoker Award nominations. Amanda lives in Kentucky with her husband and two children.

Connect with Amanda:
website: amandacrum.com
FB: mandycrum
Twitter: @MandyGCrum
IG: @amandacrumart

www.BOROUGHSPUBLISHINGGROUP.com

If you enjoyed this book, please write a review. Our authors appreciate the feedback, and it helps future readers find books they love. We welcome your comments and invite you to send them to info@boroughspublishinggroup.com.

Follow us on Facebook, Twitter and Instagram, and be sure to sign up for our newsletter for surprises and new releases from your favorite authors.

Are you an aspiring writer? Check out www.boroughspublishinggroup.com/submit and see if we can help you make your dreams come true.

Love podcasts? Enjoy ours at www.boroughspublishinggroup.com/podcast

www.ingramcontent.com/pod-product-compliance
Lightning Source LLC
Chambersburg PA
CBHW051834170626
46807CB00003B/1166